Noël in Love Copy

Gigi Hodge

Dedication

To my husband, for everything you do and especially for your two-day trek through mountains, lakes, and jungles to get my new computer!

Contents

1. Mauvaise chance [Bad Luck] — 1

2. Introducing Mrs. Richard — 7

3. Wake Up — 15

4. Save the Day — 23

5. Relationship Agreement — 31

6. Bourré — 41

7. Helping Others — 47

8. Planning and Plotting — 53

9. Thanksgiving Meeting — 59

10. Thanksgiving & Black Friday — 65

11. Inheritance Mystery — 73

12. Noël au Village — 79

13. First Gumbo — 85

14. Cooling Down = Heating Up — 91

15. Old Wounds — 99

16. Rage Decorating — 105

17.	Prison Break	111
18.	Boat Decorating	117
19.	Christmas on the Bayou	123
20.	Betrayal	131
21.	Not Betrayal	137
22.	Dance Recital	143
23.	Cajun Night Before Christmas Party	149
24.	Hero	155
25.	The Reading of the Will	161
26.	Christmas Eve	167
27.	Christmas Lovin'	173
28.	Christmas Day	181
Epilogue: King Cake		187
Also by Gigi Hodge		195
About the Author		197
Acknowledgements		199

❦

1

Mauvaise chance [Bad Luck]

Kayleigh

If I didn't have bad luck, I'd have no luck at all. No, not *la mauvaise chance*, deliberate sabotage. I took a deep breath and closed my eyes. When I opened them, I still found myself in the back of my Subaru on the lumpy foam mattress that was my makeshift bed. I hunched over, my focus alternating between my bank statement and the impressive stack of bills spread before me. I sighed with nostalgia, remembering when I lived in an apartment. Who knew an actual bed was a luxury? I selected one of the Happy Home assisted living bills. My priority was keeping my dear sister, Claire, safe and sound. After paying the bill online, I had twenty dollars to live off of for the next two weeks. *Take care of Claire and survive,* my mantra since childhood. I laid back and stared at the fairy lights I had placed around my Subaru ceiling to make urban car living seem less depressing.

Everything began unraveling the instant I resisted my uncle's wishes. The layoff, the eviction, and Claire losing her health insurance, the puzzle pieces formed a clear picture. No more excuses. He's *pas bon*, and that's the truth. I'd been pretending for ages that my uncle was just controlling, imagining that he had our best interests at heart, but these past couple of years had opened my eyes.

I called my father to see if he could help. "Dad, can you send me some cash?" While I spoke, I walked through the twenty-four-hour fitness center that served as my bathroom and showering facility. I set my backpack on the counter and glanced at my reflection. *Is my hair thinning?* I looked like crap. With dark circles under my blue eyes and my veins visible through my pale skin, I had that heroin chic look so prized in the '90s. *Must eat better.*

"I'm sorry, honey. You know your uncle controls the purse strings, and he has made it clear that giving money to you means that your mother and I can't pay our bills here." Here being their luxury condo in Florida. My parents were a kept couple. They let Nonc Bill control everything, and he kept them in booze, pickleball, and easy living. My back stiffened as I held my temper in check. Yelling at my father only caused him to hang up and pretend the call dropped.

"Yes, but part of the reason that I have so many expenses is that I'm paying Claire's medical bills, which should be your responsibility. What happened with her health insurance?" More fool me for trusting them to meet their parental obligations to Claire. As I pulled out my microfiber towel, I took a deep whiff. It still smelled clean.

"Honey, you know Bill pays for everything. Why don't you ask him? I'm sure he'll take care of you as well."

Sure, but at what price? For an instant, I wished I could be one of those cared for children whose parents handled life necessities, such as health insurance, rent, and food. That had never been my reality. I unrolled my clothes and hung them next to the shower to steam out the wrinkles. It's impossible to iron in a Subaru.

"Sorry hon. Bill's orders. We're not to send money to either of you. Why don't you talk to Bill? He manages our finances. Just let him handle yours."

Pulling my hand through my hair in frustration, I came away with a handful of blonde strands. "Dad. I talked to Nonc Bill. He expects me to date slimy Stan, who not only tried to assault me, but is also a second cousin. On top of that, I'm pretty sure that he's plotting against my friends. The criminals the Sheriff has caught all discuss a Mr. Breaux and an inheritance and the children being attacked are his children."

"Ridiculous. Bill only has one child, Brandon."

"He only has one child by marriage. DNA doesn't lie, Dad. Nonc Bill is attacking my cousins."

My father sputtered, "That's absurd. My brother is nothing if not an upstanding citizen. He runs a number of businesses and chairs numerous non-profit foundations. He's a good man, Kayleigh girl. You just need to follow his lead and you can do what you want."

"You're serious?! I should date Nonc Bill's criminal relative, to pay for your daughter's medical bills? Can you put Mom on the phone, please?"

"There is no proof that my brother is to blame. Also, your mother is busy. She's discovered her place here in Destin, and she's having tea with the head of the HOA."

Shoulders hunched, and with my stomach hollow from hunger and dread, I asked, "Okay, Dad, fess up. What does Nonc Bill have on you? You let him control all the family money and then you don't even protect your progeny from him."

Dad paused to think. A pause that I was familiar with and what I termed the prevarication pause. That is to say, the time he needed to invent a plausible lie. "I have no idea what you're talking about."

Disappointed in both his lack of support and his subpar deception techniques, I gave up on getting Dad to help me. Perhaps I could get him to relinquish one of his responsibilities.

"Let's discuss Claire. You realize that since the accident, I've taken over the responsibility of paying for the assisted living home. I understand that it would be a burden on you. For the moment, I'm handling the bills, but, if I default, you're aware that as legal guardians, the hospital can sue you for the funds. Why don't you turn over her conservatorship to me? One less thing for you to fret over in your retirement."

That suggestion was better received. Within a week, I had paperwork awarding me my sister's conservatorship in hand and hidden in my Subaru. While the public service library job didn't come with a hefty paycheck, the outstanding benefits made up for it. My chest loosened as I filled out the forms for her to be covered under my insurance. Even though I lived in my car, I found solace in knowing that Claire was protected. Once everything was official, I celebrated with a few drinks at Cowboys, our local bar. With Claire safe, I had nothing left to lose. In a moment of liquid courage, I drunk-dialed Nonc Bill to let him know I was no longer under his thumb. I forgot the old adage about not poking the sleeping bear. *My bad.*

My uncle worked fast. The next day, as I was leaving the fitness center and heading to my car for the night, I found Slimy Stan leaning up against my car. With his greasy hair, bolo tie, and used car salesman style, he sneered at me. Scoffing at my plastic bag of dirty clothes, he said, "You're a homeless bag lady. My cousin needs to pay me more to take you off the streets. At any rate, I'm here to marry you."

Yeah. That's how he greeted me. The last time I spoke with this loser, he had twisted my wrist and slapped me in the face. In hindsight, I should have pressed charges then. Now I was facing the disastrous consequences of ignoring a problem instead of confronting it. *Live and learn. I hope.*

"Stan, we don't know each other and what I do know of you I loathe, so that would be a negatory. Leave me be. There is no way in hell I'll marry you; I should've had you arrested the first time you put a hand on me. Nonc Bill tried to set me up in high school. It didn't work then and it won't work now." I pulled out my phone to dial 911.

"You would rather be homeless than marry me? You're trash and a fool." He pushed away from my Subaru and moved towards me.

I backed up. "That I won't deny. My question to you is why would you want me to marry you? Also, why would you do Nonc Bill's dirty work? That was you that organized the attack on my cousins, wasn't it?"

"My lawyers insist that I say 'no comment' to such questions. If we married, I could tell you, but since you are adamant that we don't get married, I guess I'll go with your uncle's plan B." He moved towards me. As I dialed the phone to call for help, he knocked it out of my grasp and struck me across the face. The rest was a blur. I remember slashing his cheek with my nails, content that I hadn't yet had time to trim them. Then just pain and nothing.

2

Introducing Mrs. Richard

Marc

I paced the hallway at Our Lady Hospital as I waited to check up on Kayleigh. The whiff of antiseptic spiked my impatience. I tapped my foot to the throbbing beat of the headache that was pounding in my head. The deputies that were part-time on my payroll had informed me that Kayleigh's injuries were extensive but not life-threatening. According to them, she had momentarily regained consciousness, providing enough evidence to implicate Stan. After which she slipped into unconsciousness. Something about brain swelling. My chest tightened, restricting my breathing. I needed to see her and assign guards outside her door. *Safety first. Safety Always.* However, the nurses were being difficult. I'm not a fan of difficult.

Armand phoned for a sit-rep. Renee, his wife, was the one that alerted us to the attack on Kayleigh. "Did the hospital call her parents?"

While taking a turn outside to clear my mind, I filled him in on the details. "Based on the bug that I placed at the front desk, the parents aren't answering. Hold on, let me listen ... Oh, crap, her next of kin is her uncle William Breaux. They're getting his number."

Armand's agitation was palpable. "I don't care if we have no direct evidence of his guilt. You gotta stop this, Marc."

"I'm on it. I'll call you back once it's resolved." With my jaw set, I clicked off on my phone and called my law team. Within five minutes, they had delivered the signed and notarized documents to me. As I approached the front desk, I commanded they must, under no circumstances, contact her uncle. That the ex-boyfriend was in custody and he had implicated the uncle in the attack. I gave them my paperwork, and they showed me to her room.

Kayleigh was a mess. A tiny blond crumpled on that hospital bed. Her face was so swollen and covered in bruises that it made it difficult to distinguish her features. Her pouty and snarky rosebud mouth now sported a split lip. Grinding my back teeth, I took a deep breath through my nose to dissipate the heat that rushed through me. I always thought of Kayleigh as a rabid little bunny, a rabid bunny that smelled as if she rolled in a field of lavender. No whiff of lavender today, just the odor of antiseptic and bleach. Movement in my periphery indicated another patient in her room. I buzzed the nurse. No one came. I buzzed again.

After a lapse of ten minutes, a nurse arrived. With a nod of my chin, I gestured towards the privacy screen next to Kayleigh's bed. "Can that patient be transferred? I need a private room, please, for my wife."

"That's not how it works, Mr. Breaux. Besides, this gentleman is just waiting for his discharge paperwork." She pointed to the older man who had peeked through a gap in the screen. He was buttoning his dress shirt, getting ready to leave.

He appeared innocuous enough, but I was taking no chances. "Mr. Richard," I corrected the nurse.

She glanced down at her clipboard. "Her ID said that she's a Breaux."

"We're newlyweds. She hasn't had time to change her documentation to reflect her new status. I'll pay for the private room. She's a victim of a criminal attack. I'm a security professional. Trust me when I tell you, I need to reduce the number of people who have access to my wife. Please, just ask your patient to move."

"Nurse," the man said through the screen. "I've no problem moving. You just take care of your little wifey. I believe she's suffering. She was moaning earlier. I tried the call button, but no one came."

Kayleigh moaned. Making my way towards her, I reached out and laid a proprietary hand on her arm. Normally, she was a colossal pain in my *tchu*, but today she was a sorry sight, covered in bruises, battered, and wincing with every movement. I gave an accusatory look at the nurse.

She stiffened. "I'm sorry, Mr. Richard, but we're short staffed. We're trying to get to as many patients as we can."

I pulled out my phone. "Not a problem. Take care of her immediate pain, now; I'll provide more staff so you can tend to your other patients." Then I turned and walked around the screen to the gentleman who was giving up his bed. "Thank you." I handed him my card. "I owe you a favor."

He pushed back the card. "I don't need a favor. Let's just make sure your little lady is safe."

I tucked it into his shirt. "You never know. You might find me to be a valuable connection." He smiled and nodded. Kayleigh moaned again. Turning to the nurse while keeping my temper in check, I lowered my voice. "Can you *please* do something for her pain?"

She sighed, walked over, and fiddled with one of the IV fluid bag valves. "That should help for now. She's a fighter."

"She's a pistol." I brushed blond strands from her eyes and a clump of it came off in my hands. "Often doling out more spunk than I can handle."

The nurse averted her gaze, but I saw her lip curl. "She's undernourished and underweight. Your wife has not been taking care of herself. Is she on some kind of fad diet? Has she been showing signs of anorexia? We added electrolytes, alimentation, and essential vitamins to her fluids. We need some tests before we can do more. Regarding the additional help, I'm not certain you can or will be allowed to help with that, Mr. Richard."

"It's about to go over your pay grade, darling. Just take the extra help and smile. I'm not accusing you, just as I'm sure that you are not accusing me of anything. I have this covered." Within fifteen minutes, my private physician and nurse were evaluating Kayleigh's condition. As they tended to Kayleigh, I carefully evaluated the situation. How could a pipsqueak like Stan Breaux have left Kayleigh for dead and then penetrated the security defense system I'd designed for my friend Armand? He couldn't have … not without help. Only one other person had the administrative access to do this. My fists clenched.

I was trying to get comfortable on the Spartan couch in Kayleigh's room when my phone buzzed.

Armand: I think you have a mole

I nodded, because that was my take as well. The sabotage was a gut punch, but thankfully no one I cared for had died because of my misplaced trust. I turned to examine Kayleigh. Since I'd met her as a pushy EMT, she'd always reminded me of a rabid bunny. Adorable, but with teeth. She never put up with any nonsense. This was the reason why she thrived as a librarian and integrated well into our Krewe alongside educators Renee and Shell. Now she looked beaten and helpless. I was massaging my forehead with my fingers when Armand texted again.

Armand: A mole who knew how to cut off your security system and all the camera angles.

I'm on that too. Just got into Kayleigh's room. She put up quite a fight. She's gonna be in recovery for a while.

Armand: How did you get into her room so quickly?

I pulled an Armand.

Armand: What's an Armand? What did I do?

You can ask Kayleigh Richard when she wakes up.

Armand: You're so dead. How did you get a marriage license so quickly?

Where there's a will…

Armand: You mean where there's a ton of cash?

I'm a capitalist. You know that.

I waited a moment for him to respond.

> Armand: Gotta go. Renee needs me. Do *not* leave Kayleigh unguarded & find that mole.

> Not a chance and the mole is already found. Just devising the appropriate punishment.

> Armand: Wait on that. We might be able to use him.

Feeling twitchy, my nostrils flared as I texted my lawyer, Hercule Trahan. He set in motion the steps necessary to protect my company as I got rid of my mole. Afterwards, I altered every passcode, making sure that only I had access to them. If Judas asked, I'd tell him we were updating the software as a precaution against a virus.

Meanwhile, we had to move Kayleigh to a safer location. Her apartment was not an option. I'd sent my PI there to dig up answers. When he came by with pictures not of her apartment, but of her car, I realized Kayleigh had been hiding some hard truths. The puzzle pieces clicked into place and the malnutrition now made sense. I studied her pale complexion. She'd be going back to live in her car, to live on the streets, over my dead body. Plus, the car was trashed. Stan must have destroyed it before he headed over to *Mes Rêves*, Armand's and Renee's farm. Kayleigh needed protection, whether she liked it or not. I grinned, knowing she would, without a doubt, *not* want my protection. Too bad for her. Still, one can never be too safe. I texted my lawyer to draw up an agreement for her to sign once she recovered. I was determined to protect Kayleigh, but past betrayals made me cautious. Despite her being tight with my friends and Armand's cousin, this interaction was a simple business arrangement. My protection for my peace of mind, a win/win for me. If Kayleigh wanted to complain, she could damn well wake up to do that.

$$3$$

Wake Up

Kayleigh

I awoke in a strange place to the sound of Mariah Carey's "All I Want for Christmas" and the scent of, I sniffed, lavender and pumpkin pie. I inhaled deeply, breathing in the delightful aroma, then I opened my eyes and blinked. Based on the machines I was hooked up to, it was apparent that I was in a hospital, but the *Southern Living*-inspired decor added unexpected warmth and charm. After shaking my head to clear it, I took stock of my surroundings. The room was so perfect. I imagined a local realtor extolling the property features.

"Why look at this expansive bedroom," she drawled. *"With enormous windows that filter in a ton of light. The pale periwinkle on the walls brings out the wood tones in the floor and the mid-century modern furniture. Large enough for this king size bed, minus, of course, the bedraggled stranger currently curled up on it."* The realtor in my head was a *putain*. [bitch]

A nurse, or possibly a doctor, a medical professional, walked in and stopped mid-stride.

"You're awake," she stated.

"Yes."

She ran out of the room. *Curiouser and curiouser.* With the machines humming and beeping around me, and the apparent medical professional, I decided it might be wise to assess my physical and mental states.

Hello, can I understand me? My English-speaking brain worked. *Et asteur Il faut essayer mon français.* Okay, my French brain worked as well. Scanning the room, I listened to the sound of the machines. My eyes and ears were in perfect working order ... Check. Next I tried out my appendages. Everything appeared to be intact, lethargic, but intact.

As I was moving my left hand, I noticed the glimmer. I moved my hand closer, but that brought it out of focus. So, I'm still far-sighted. As I extended my arm to focus, a gorgeous ring came into view. A Georgian sapphire and diamond ... *No!* I turned it in the light and saw the clasp. Upon further investigation, I found the secret hidden compartment. It was a poison ring. I had a collection of poison rings I had purchased at Renaissance fairs. Cheap silver rings that inevitably turned my fingers green. This one was not cheap. It was the real deal. I held it up to the light. Inside, etched on the shiny gold band, was the inscription *à Kayleigh.* But how did it get there? And who gave it to me, and why was it on my left ring finger? My heart rate picked up, not Stan. If he had trapped me in marriage, he wouldn't have bothered with a ring, much less engrave it in French.

The nurse-doctory person rushed back in with another nurse-doctory person. I decided to call them Nurse One and Nurse Two. They were checking the machine for readouts and straightening the room. If they were doctors, I'd re-name them. Since they were doing a ton of work to make me comfortable, I stuck with the assumption that they were nurses.

"Hello, Mrs. Richard, how are you feeling?" Nurse One asked.

I turned to check if someone else, this Mrs. Richard, was somewhere behind me. There was no one there. "Are you talking to me?"

Nurse One nodded and marked something on her clipboard. "Yes, it appears you may still have some lingering memory issues from the attack."

"No, I remember the attack. *T'tchu,* Stan, ambushed me at my car. First he insulted me, then he asked me to marry him, and, finally, when I turned his sorry ass down, he attacked me. I was able to get some good licks in, though. I hope they put the *fils d' putain* [son of a bitch] under the jail."

Nurse Two shook her head. "Poor thing is talking gibberish. She'll need a brain scan." Nurse One sniggered at that.

I rolled my eyes at her and bit my cheek. "*Américain?*"

Nurse One nodded. "*Ouais, d'*Ohio."

I turned to Nurse Two. "You're a long way from Ohio. It wasn't gibberish. It was French. Why are you calling me Mrs. Richard? My name is Kayleigh Breaux."

"Not according to our records. They say you are Mrs. Kayleigh Richard."

I glanced at my ring and frowned. "Exactly how long have I been unconscious?"

Nurse One told me, "About a month."

I stiffened in a panic. "A month since Stan attacked me? What? No." The machines attached to my arm began emitting a cacophony of frantic beeps.

Marc Richard, clearly up to something, ran in, like a frantic Clark Kent, trying to hide Superman's cape. "Kayleigh, my dear! You're awake." He came over and kissed my cheek. "Do you need help getting up?" His large, warm hand gripped my shoulder.

I pulled away and squinted. "I need help understanding—"

"—Of course you do, sweetheart." His grip tightened on my shoulder. *Okay, I'm not couillon.* Only an idiot would miss that this was a ruse. A ruse he clearly wanted me to play along with.

I gave him my patented I'm-gonna-kill-you-dead smile and pierced him with my baby blues. "Yes, please, darling." I took his offered arm and dug my nails into his forearms. Those forearms that I ogled on the sly. His hazel eyes barely blinked at the pain behind those wire-rimmed glasses he wore. I was almost positive I drew blood. *Serves him right.*

He turned to the nurses. "Will you please give my wife and me a moment alone?"

I could play along. "Yes, my *husband* and I have ... issues to discuss."

"Understood," Nurse One said, but Nurse Two looked skeptical. Nurse One pulled her out the door.

Once they had closed the door, I turned on Marc. "What the hell, Marc?"

Marc put his finger to his lips. He pulled out a small electronic gadget from his pocket and scanned. Its light illuminated three times as he circled the room.

He disconnected my IV and threw me the fluffiest robe I'd ever worn and a pair of even fluffier bunny slippers. Apparently, I had woken up in an alternate reality. A parallel universe wherein I am married to Marc *Couillon* Richard. Perhaps I should just go back to bed. He opened the sheers from the windows, and I saw that they were, in fact, French doors. I peered through the glass. The doors led to a patio and a garden, the most amazing garden I'd ever seen. It exploded with a profusion of flowers and, when Marc opened the doors, it smelled better than the expensive trendy perfumes my mother wore.

I couldn't keep the grin off my face. "Is that a labyrinth?" I read the sign on the garden gate. "The Secret Garden?"

"Yes, to both. I built it for Sofia. Her room is next to yours. Apparently, a certain radical librarian got her hooked-on Frances Hodgson Burnett's book, *The Secret Garden*, and I must pay the price." He opened the French doors for me before running his hand through his sable hair.

My grin widened, and I pulled the gate open. I stole inside the garden without another word. Sofia sat on a cushioned bench reading, her dark curls making a curtain around her face. She lifted her head when she heard the gate. Grinning, she showcased her missing teeth. "Ms. Kayleigh! You're awake." She ran towards me and hugged me.

The impact was painful, but worth it. Sofia was book obsessed and thus a favorite at the library. I hugged her back and breathed in her sweet smell of baby shampoo and Downy. "Sofia, is this your garden? If I had known you had a secret reading garden, I would have come over sooner."

She giggled. "This is the best part of my house, Ms. Kayleigh. Are you hungry? Do you like beignets? Chef Agnès makes them every Friday to celebrate the coming of the weekend."

"Aww, that's fun. Isn't it a school day? Shouldn't you be in school?"

"Daddy let me take off today. In each season, he lets me take a day off. We call it Sofia-day and I get to do whatever I want. How are you doing? Daddy said you got hurt, and you needed to recolor here? But you've been asleep for a long time. I have some coloring books you can use to recolor. You can even use my good box of crayons."

I pressed my lips together and hugged her tighter. Pain be damned. "That's very generous and sounds like fun, but I think he might have meant recover?"

Marc brushed his hand over Sofia's head. "Yes. That's exactly what she's supposed to be doing. Sofia, why don't you get us some beignets to share? We can have a secret garden picnic."

I softened, looking at Sofia. "Sofia, *ma hérie*, beignets sound delicious. I want at least three. Will you fix me a plate?"

"Okay, Ms. Kayleigh." Sofia hugged her dad and then hugged me one more time before she skipped toward the French doors next to mine. She was such a sweetie. I don't know how she was raised by *that* man.

She called over her shoulder. "See you soon, Ms. Kayleigh. The kids at the library will be glad to know that you're up and about. Maybe we could do story-time this weekend? We all miss that."

I said "Absolutely."

While Marc, the control freak, called out, "We'll see how she's feeling."

After Sofia skipped off for sustenance, Marc turned to me. "How about we stretch your legs and walk around the garden, or do you need to sit on the bench?" He reached out and tipped up my chin.

I batted away his hands. "Hands off! I need answers, not coddling."

"I'm looking at your bruises. They were deep. It's been a month and they're still there. Also, we must check and make sure you have no long-term issues after that coma."

"Coma, the nurses said something about me being unconscious for a month."

"What do you remember?" Marc sat on one side of the bench, and I sat on the other.

"I remember drunk-dialing Nonc Bill the night before the attack, and gloating about how he couldn't control me. The next day, after my fitness routine, I headed to my car to … to go home … and there was Creepy Stan, awaiting my arrival. He disparaged me, called me names, and then, like the Casanova he is, asked me to marry him."

Marc snorted. "*Couillon.*"

"Right?! When I refused his offer of marriage, he beat the crap out of me. I remember being glad I forgot to cut my nails. I hope I slashed up his cheek, but good." I cringed, rubbing the side of my face and my torso, remembering the blows.

"You did, and his DNA under your nails sealed his fate. Also, before you went down for the count, you named him as your attacker."

With a shake of my head, I said, "I have no recollection of that, but yay me!"

Marc's lip curled into a sneer as he remarked, "The *fils d'putain* is singing like a canary. Your uncle is under investigation. Let's hope that keeps him busy."

I scoffed at that. "We can hope, but don't hold your breath." Then I remembered why I had called Nonc Bill, and I stood abruptly. "My car. I need to see my car. Did they impound it?"

"No, it's stored in one of my outbuildings."

"I have to see it now!" The world started to swim, and I swayed.

Marc grasped my shoulders to steady me. "Okay, okay. Let's get you dressed and fed and then we can head out to see it," he said. "But, word of warning, it's trashed."

My eyes met his through the fog that was whirling around me. "What do you mean trashed?"

"I had my people go through it when we towed it here. Just to get some of your clothes."

I colored and cringed. "You had no right to snoop through my car!" At least the rage had dissipated my nausea.

"The police already snooped through it. I have some crime scene photos of your car when they began their investigation. You want to see them?" I nodded, and he brought up the images on his phone.

"Let me see that." I plucked the phone out of Marc's hand and examined the photos around my make-shift bed. I stilled and attempted to breathe, trying not to panic. It didn't work. I rocked back and forth, gasping for breath. *It might be too late.*

Marc sat me back down on the bench and called to his staff for a paper bag. When it arrived, he handed it to me. "What's wrong?" he asked, as I breathed into the bag.

"I think ... Stan took something ... something important." I explained between breaths.

"What?"

I shook my head. This was not his problem. *My problem, my responsibility.* "Nevermind, it's not important."

"You just said it *was* important."

As I fell silent, the sound of Marc tapping on his phone filled the air. When he finished, he smiled at me, but the smile did not reach his eyes. It was a look I knew well. Ever since I joined his friends' group, I knew when I saw that look that Mr. Richard was up to something. Surely there were no more surprises life could throw at me. *It's not paranoia if the world is actually out to get you.*

4

Save the Day

Marc

Kayleigh dressed in a green dress and high blonde pony tail, only underlining my unwelcome Tinker Bell fantasies. Once she had eaten breakfast, she was flagging, but stubborn. Her eyes were at half mast, and she was yawning.

I stated the obvious. "You need to rest before we go."

Her deep blue eyes flashed from half-mast to frowning. "You're not the boss of me. I can head out on my own, just point to the building."

In disagreement, I shook my head. "'Fraid not. You only recently awoke from a coma. You shouldn't be running around the property. The doctors haven't cleared you yet."

She poked my chest with her finger. "You're the one that told me to walk with you—"

"—Because I needed to speak with you, out of the prying ears of others."

Kayleigh got in my face and lowered her voice. "You can take me there or I'll wander around your property asking for directions from everyone. Your choice."

I shrugged. "Negatory. Every person here takes orders from me. Don't make me lock you in your room."

"I'd like to see you try!" She gave as good as she got.

Sighing, I tried to reason with her. "Just humor me. You look exhausted. It's your first day. Take a quick nap and I'll arrange for everything while you sleep."

"I'll come and read to you," Sofia said, wandering into the kitchen, wanting to diffuse the tension.

I smiled at Sophia, my little peacemaker, while Kayleigh's face softened with affection.

"Fine," Kayleigh growled.

Sofia took her hand as they walked back to her room. A few minutes later, I heard Sofia reading to her through the door. Sofia left the room a few moments later. "Shh, Ms. Kayleigh's tired, Daddy."

I nodded and organized the sortie while I waited. After Kayleigh had taken a quick nap, she looked rested and had more color in her cheeks. She still was dangerously thin. I'd neglected to notice before, back when we would spar, but it was evident now. Kayleigh hadn't been taking care of herself. After seeing where she'd been living for the past few months, I had a better understanding of why. Not wanting her to overdo it, I insisted on a wheelchair. I knew that this would be a stressful visit. We wheeled her towards the outbuilding, where my team had securely stored her car. Remnants of the crime scene police tape dangled from the rear hatch door.

"I had my men clean up some, but they had no idea what went where. It seems like either Stan wanted to make sure you had no place to live, or he was searching for something. Any insight into why this happened?"

She shot up out of the wheelchair and began digging under her mattress. "No, I ... my papers. They aren't here. Dammit! How did he find them?"

I touched her shoulder. "Find what? Kayleigh, explain, please."

"You should've brought me here right away. He might not have gotten them." She was in panic mode now, pounding on my shoulders.

"Kayleigh, darlin', the car was ransacked over a month ago. Whatever is missing was taken then." She sobbed. "Kayleigh, please, use your words."

"He took the papers." Those were the only words I could discern from her sobs.

"What papers? Why would anyone take your papers?" I asked.

"To give me no choice. Claire!" She continued to sob. I reached for her shoulders, but she brushed me away.

"Your uncle took them?"

She nodded, unable to speak. After a moment, she collected herself. "I need to go. Can you drive me to the Happy Place assisted living home?"

I pulled out my keys. "Yes. I'll give you a ride to wherever you need to go. En route you can tell me what the paperwork said and who you filed it with. If there was a legal document, it should be filed somewhere."

I called up Kevin Babineaux on speaker phone. "Kevin, we need help with a legal matter."

En route, Kayleigh gave Kevin the details regarding her conservatorship of her sister. He contacted the lawyer who had helped Kayleigh.

Kayleigh explained. "My uncle had been holding her care over my head. In October, I succeeded in getting my parents to sign her conservatorship over to me. I'm clueless about what my uncle has on my father, but whatever it is, my father can't or won't help me."

"I'll figure that out as well. In the meantime, Kevin will meet us at the Happy Place home with the official documents."

When we arrived there, she asked the nurse at reception to see her sister.

The nurse on duty shook her head. "I'm sorry ma'am, you've been taken off the approved visitor's list."

"On whose authority?" I asked.

"Her uncle, Mr. Breaux, was quite adamant," the nurse responded.

"Mr. Breaux is not the conservator of my sister, I am!" Kayleigh insisted.

"He had documents showing that he was the conservator."

As if on cue, Kevin walked in, his hands holding papers aloft. "Interesting, because I have these official and notarized documents that were signed by a judge, giving Mrs. Richard here, conservatorship. You, of course, followed hospital protocol and made copies of Mr. Breaux's papers?"

"Well ... ah...." The nurse hedged.

"I'm sorry. What's your name?" Kevin asked her.

"Sally Jones," she answered.

"Ms. Jones, that's a serious lapse in hospital protocol. Before transferring responsibility for someone's care, it's essential to verify their legal authority. Now, these papers include the legally filed conservatorship papers of Mrs. Richard, her marriage license showing that she recently married Mr. Richard, and an injunction against the hospital for any change of status. We need to see Ms. Claire Breaux now. Furthermore, we need to be made aware of *any* changes in care that Mr. Breaux *illegally* asked you to do and that you might've *illegally* complied with."

"He had us take out her feeding tube."

Kayleigh moaned, "No!" Her breath shuddered as she tried to get control of her emotions.

Grinding my teeth, heat flashed through my system, and I exploded. "*You,* without *any* legal authority and without following *protocol*, were willing to allow a woman to *die*? You get her food, right *now,* and get your legal team down here this instant."

"I didn't know!" Nurse Jones backpedaled.

My patience had run thin, so I savaged her. "Next time someone asks you to *murder* someone, perhaps ask some questions. Kevin, what are my options?"

Kevin looked at his phone. "Well, the home is affiliated with Our Lady Hospital."

With a nod, I told Kevin, "Five minutes. Tell them that is how much time I'll give them to get someone to contact me or I stop payment on their burn unit check."

"Now, take us to my sister-in-law and she better have a feeding tube in before we get there."

"Yes, sir," the nurse said. "Follow me."

Kayleigh gave me a hard hug and then followed after the nurse. I mouthed 'thank you' to Kevin.

He nodded and dialed a number on his phone. "I need to report a crime."

Leaving Kevin to it, I followed Kayleigh. It might be a temporary marriage, but I believe I had definitely earned the right to meet my new sister-in-law. When I got to Claire's room, Kayleigh was already holding her hand.

"I'm so sorry, sweetie." Kayleigh kissed her sister's cheek. The room was bleak and dirty.

Claire's big brown eyes stared into Kayleigh's blue ones. "Nonc Bill said you turned over my care to him, and then they stopped feeding me."

Kayleigh denied that. "No, he stole my conservatorship paperwork and illegally got them to stop feeding you. I'm sorry, Claire, I was in a coma. I didn't know what had happened."

"In a coma? You were hurt? Nobody told me. What's happening, Kayleigh? First our accident, then you get hurt." Claire blinked in confusion. Dark circles shone through her translucent skin, and her short, light brown hair appeared unkempt.

Kayleigh leaned down to kiss Claire's cheek. "Nonc Bill sent someone to force me to comply. I did not."

"It's like he doesn't know you at all." Claire smirked, showing a glimpse of a familiar attitude.

Okay, now I see the resemblance. I snorted from the doorway. "Yeah, one word that doesn't describe our Kayleigh is compliant." Claire chuckled. I entered Claire's line of sight. "Hello Claire. Can you tell us how long you've been without food?"

Claire glanced at Kayleigh, who nodded. "You can trust him. He's a *tchu*, but he's safe."

Claire grinned. "Pushy, determined, and hot. You must be Marc Richard. Kayleigh has complained about you before."

At Kayleigh's gasp of outrage, I smirked at her. "Hot, huh?"

Kayleigh sniffed. "Empirically, your features fit in the *pho* proportions, the Greek formula for beauty. You don't make me gag when I see you." Her lip quirked up.

Claire chuckled. "That's high praise from Kay Kay."

"And yet, none of that answers my question. How long since you last ate?"

She winked at Kayleigh. "He is determined. I haven't had a feeding tube in two weeks, but I've been eating every day. The tube was because I needed more nutrition than I could eat. I can chew and swallow. One nurse has been sneaking me food. She brought me broth, and applesauce, and popsicles."

I nodded. "Which nurse?"

Claire's jaw tightened. "I don't want to get her in trouble."

I pulled out my phone. "You won't. You'll make sure that she has a nice cushy job as your private nurse."

Claire nodded at that. "Jeanne Richard."

I chuckled.

"What?" Kayleigh asked.

"That's my cousin, distant. She's good people and has already worked for my company, so adding her to my payroll will be simple. I'm texting her now."

Once we got Claire situated with Jeanne as her private nurse and Kayleigh set up a schedule to visit with her every week, Kevin and I put the fear of God into the administration, and we made sure that only Jeanne and another of my private nurses cared for Claire. It still made me nervous to keep her at the facility, but I needed to remodel my home to ensure it had wheelchair access before we could bring her home. I might not be permanently married to Kayleigh, but I could make sure when she left that she and her sister were in a better place.

5

Relationship Agreement

Kayleigh

After Marc rescued Claire, my days fell into a comfortable rhythm. I got into a groove. He still annoyed me to no end with his high-handed ways, but since his high-handedness saved my sister, I tried to hold my tongue most of the time. Plus, I had other things to do. I started back at the library, but there was still no way to get my EMT job back. Since I wasn't paying for food or gasoline, and Claire's medical bills disappeared after Marc's threatened litigation, I could live off the one salary. Every day, Sofia and I ate breakfast and had coffee with Marc. Well, coffee milk for Sofia. After breakfast, Sofia and I walked in the garden and read at the outdoor folly Marc had constructed for her reading pleasure. It kinda looked like a Greek temple, a greenhouse, and a gazebo had gotten together and had a child. Sofia's folly was whimsical, which contradicted my initial assessment of my temporary husband.

In the afternoon, I'd return from visiting Claire, whose health had improved dramatically. Once Sofia finished school or dance class, we started our afternoon routine. We began by going over our holiday plans at the kitchen table. We listed them, added bullets of included activities, and posted them on the fridge. Then it was reading time again. We gathered snacks and took the snack and our books back out to the folly. I also read to her every night before bed. *Mathilda* was our current book. Sophia was a hoot. I'd so miss this once Marc and I got out of our fake marriage. Which I guess wasn't fake. I mean, there was paperwork with my signature on it. I didn't ask how he got my signature when I was unconscious. I was just relieved, knowing that I had escaped the clutches of my conniving uncle.

One evening, I left Sofia's room after she gave me a big hug and headed to the kitchen for a relaxing mint tisane. Marc was already there, munching on holiday cookies.

"Sofia was saying how she wanted to see the Christmas bonfires this year. Do you think you can talk her out of it? It would mean us having to reserve a hotel suite. I don't like driving that far with Sofia in the dark."

"I can find some other activity to entice her." I put the teakettle on the stove to heat and turned to study him. "You're a very protective father."

Marc pulled out two cups and held out the tea organizer. "And that's bad?"

I chose a mint tea, putting the bag in my cup to wait for the hot water. "That's good and oddly sweet."

He selected a packet of matcha green tea. *Blech!* "I'm a sweet guy."

I snorted at that.

"What? I am." He sifted a half-teaspoon of matcha powder into his cup.

"I suppose when you want to be. But you have a mean and an annoying side as well."

"I'm multi-faceted." At that instant, dimples emerged. I had known the man for years. Why had I never noticed them? Probably because all he's ever done is frown at me.

I narrowed my eyes at his charming dimples and poured steaming water in both our cups. He stopped me when I'd covered the powder with water.

"Let's talk about your future." Marc pulled out a small brush to whisk his tea.

"I can't stay here anymore. I don't take charity." My heart lurched at the thought of missing reading with Sofia, and I had no idea how I could care for Claire, but I'd find a way.

When his matcha was frothy, Marc motioned to the teakettle with his chin. I poured him more hot water. He held up his hand to show that was enough water and said, "Why not? It's no hardship on me."

"Sofia is starting to get ideas." *I'm starting to get ideas.* My gaze strayed to his muscled forearms. Such well-defined muscles were distracting. I peered up at Marc. Luckily, he was impervious to my forearm lust.

He inhaled the scent of his matcha tea before he sampled it. "Perfect." He enjoyed another taste before he set his cup on the counter and considered me. "I tell you what. I will give you a nice clean divorce—"

"—We shouldn't even be married."

"That was to protect you from your uncle, who we suspect is trying to hurt your cousins and put you under his thumb. Just hear me out." He moved the honey bear closer to my untouched tea.

"Fine. What's your plan?" I squeezed a generous dollop of honey into my cup, watching it ooze and swirl into the hot liquid. To be at my best and defeat my uncle, I had to overcome my calorie deficit and be in peak physical condition.

"I'll give you a nice, clean divorce. Pay for the best lawyer for you so you can clean me out—"

"—I don't want to clean you out, Marc. I a ... a... appreciate what you have done for me."

He pressed his lips together. "That was hard for you, wasn't it?"

"Shut up! I changed my mind. I'm going to clean you out and put everything in a trust for Sofia." I narrowed my eyes at him. The duplicitous *tchu*.

Marc guffawed. "Can I just *tell* you my plan? How about you let me talk uninterrupted for five minutes?"

"Fine." I took a sip of my sweet, soothing tea. Hot tea, running water, and a secret garden. *This was the good life.* I sighed. "Go ahead."

"And you won't interrupt?" His eyebrow lifted.

"I make no promises." I twirled my hand in front of him. "You may begin."

"I want you to stay through Christmas."

"What? Why?" My mind flashed to the comfort of my room, Claire's care, and my now destroyed Subaru. Staying would be easy, but my throat clogged at the thought of the control I'd lose.

He held up his hands. "We are in the middle of something here, Kayleigh. If you're here, you'll be safe. I have security."

"Your security is not foolproof, buster."

"No, but I can protect you here more easily than if you and Claire are living in your trashed car." Following that hit of truth, Marc handed me a document.

The document was awash in legalese. I frowned. "What's this?"

Marc's hand enveloped the cup as he raised it to his mouth. Then he said, "A relationship agreement."

I flipped it opened and smirked. "You mean, like Amy and Sheldon in the Big Bang?"

"No, like a legal agreement outlining our roles, the benefits, and consequences of doing what we say we will do or not. It's standard operating procedure around here. This way I ensure that anyone I'm seeing, or in your case temporarily married to, has clarity in their role, and I protect Sofia."

"And yourself, no doubt, I get it. A quid pro quo with no emotional attachment." At Marc's nod, my stomach sank, but I didn't know why. "Hold on." I grabbed up Marc's phone from the counter and dialed Kevin Babineaux on speaker. "Kevin, it's me, Kayleigh."

"Hey there, Cuz! What's up?" Kevin answered.

I cocked my head. "Are we cousins?"

"Well, the *Littles* are my cousins via adoption and you are their first cousin. It's complicated, but yeah, you're family. So Cuz, what can I do for you?"

I smiled at that. "Well, *Cuz*, I have a legal agreement I need you to look over."

"Do you mean Marc's relationship agreement?" Kevin asked.

My eye flicked from the phone to Marc and back. I hesitated. "Yes, how did you guess?"

"He had me examine it and make sure it was fair, overly fair to you. My suggestion is you sign it. If you stay until Christmas, you get your freedom, a trust fund, and a yearly substantial donation to the library. It's a more than fair deal, Kayleigh. Plus, Marc will keep you safe. "

Ugh! I'm surrounded by controlling men! "And if I don't stay or if I leave early?"

"Then he just adds time for you to stay longer. There are no financial penalties on your end. He, however, doubles his trust to you if he boots you out early."

"Is that a fact?" A snide smile spread across my face. *Not a complete loss of control.* "So, ideally I just have to be such a pain in his *tchu* that he kicks me out, and I get more money." I turned to Marc. "You didn't think this through, Mr. Richard."

Kevin chuckled. "I warned him you might see that as a viable option."

Marc shrugged. "I believe I'll grow on you and besides, Sofia always wants to do more for the holidays, but that's my busiest time. Having someone here to hang out with her will be so good for her."

I scanned the contract. "So, I stay until December 25th, Christmas, and then I can leave?"

"January 6th, Epiphany," Marc corrected.

I pursed my lips. "Fine, but I want the biggest cream cheese stuffed king cake from Kellers on that 12th day of Christmas."

Kevin laughed, "Cuz, I already wrote that into the agreement. Renee said they were your favorite. I gotta go. Call if you need any revisions made, but I'm telling you, it's a sweet deal. As an added benefit, your family won't worry about you as much because you'll be safe with Marc in his Fortress of Solitude."

"Except for Claire, my family couldn't care less about me," I told him.

"Hey, Cuz, we're your family now and I promise that Armand, my brothers, and I were very worried about you," Kevin said.

Blinking back tears, I nodded. "Thanks for caring. I'll talk to you later, Cuz." Hanging up with Kevin, I turned to Marc. "Give me a pen." He handed me his fancy Mont Blanc pen, and I grabbed it up along with the document.

Marc nodded. "Excellent. Let's talk Thanksgiving."

I held up my hand. "Don't rush your fences. I haven't signed anything yet, but I'll think about it. Besides, Thanksgiving is Armand and Renee's wedding."

With a shake of his head, Marc said, "No, their wedding is three days before Thanksgiving. Thanksgiving is late this year. I spoke to the whole Krewe. Thanksgiving will be here. My house is the safest place, and I have the best security."

"What would you need me to do for Thanksgiving? You realize I'm a terrible cook, right?" I added more hot water to my now tepid tea.

"I have a chef, Chef Agnès. I just need you and Sofia to plan, as Sof would say, a splendiferous Thanksgiving feast."

"Turducken, will for sure be on the menu." My mouth watered at all the possibilities. Before the attack, I'd been living on canned beans and peanut butter sandwiches.

"I wouldn't expect it not to be. Now sign the document. Ah! Sofia!" Marc's eyes were focused behind me.

Sofia was waiting at the door. Her spidey sense had drawn her out of bed, and she knew that something important was happening in the house. "Yes, Daddy?"

"Can you help Ms. Kayleigh plan a splendiferous Thanksgiving feast?"

Sofia grinned. "Of course." She ran over and hugged me. Marc's secret 'control-Kayleigh' weapon.

Mission accomplished, he grinned. "Thanks Sof. Now, back to bed with you."

Sofia ran to Marc, kissed him on the cheek, and then ran back to her room. I picked up my cup, the pen, and the relationship agreement, and headed to bed.

Marc heaved a sigh and called after me. "Sign the damn document, Kayleigh."

I shook my head as I walked out of the kitchen. "It is a legal document, Mr. Richard. I would be remiss if I signed any legal agreement without reading it thoroughly first."

"Your lawyer said it was fine, Mrs. Richard. You know, your problem is that you are too *tête dure* and refuse help when you need it."

"Do not." I stomped down the hall towards my room.

He followed me. "Do, too."

I gave him one more. "Do not." Then I slammed my bedroom door.

Marc called through my door. "Do, too. You're a child."

I opened my door and leaned forward, my breath on his lips. "And good night to you too, old man."

"Hey, I'm not that much older than you!"

"Keep telling yourself that." I slammed my door once more and grinned.

Tossing and turning, I struggled against the hands that were on my throat as I reached up and scratched at him. I woke up in a cold sweat, and I must have screamed because Marc and his men had barged into my room.

Marc rubbed my shoulder. "Kayleigh, are you okay?"

I rubbed my temple. My headache throbbed in sync with my racing heart. This was not the time to play damsel in distress. I crossed my arms over my chest. "I'm fine."

Marc grinned, his heretofore unknown dimple making an appearance. "You're stubborn, not the same thing." Which was so annoying because I was positive I told him the same exact thing when I treated him for a concussion a while back. "Didn't the nurses explain that you needed to watch out for headaches with your brain injury? Don't you have a headache?" His hands kept rubbing circles on my shoulder and back.

My hand moved away from my temple. "Yes, but I'm an EMT. I can tell if something's wrong."

"So, you understand you need to tell someone if you are dizzy or have blurred vision?"

"I understand." Annoyed, I shook off his hand and turned to glare at him. I nearly swallowed my tongue when I saw he was only wearing boxers.

"And that if you experience dizziness, confusion, or become easily angered, you will inform me immediately and we'll go to the hospital."

I was feeling a tad dizzy, but I'm pretty sure Marc's bare chest, dimples, and nerdy glasses were to blame. I covered my discomfort the only way I knew how, with pure snark. "Of course. Although around you, I stay perpetually angry."

Marc smirked. "Talk about. The issue will be, can I tell the difference between your normal anger and a TBI induced anger? From what I can tell, outrage is your natural state."

I gave him my sweet eyes. "Only when I'm interacting with you. You inspire rage. If I get mad at someone else, then you'll know."

He snorted, then scanned me from my head to my toes. I hid my hands because they were still shaking. His eyes focused on my neck, where my pulse jack-hammered erratically.

With a lift of his chin, he sent his men away. "So, let's talk about the nightmare and the screaming."

"I didn't wake Sofia, did I?" I turned to our shared wall.

Marc chuckled. "My little goth sleeps like the dead. Fitting, really. About those nightmares. How often have you been having them?"

With a shrug of my shoulders, I downplayed everything. "It's just me reliving the attack. No big deal."

He nodded. "So, every night." He sat his near naked body next to me and patted my leg. *What was that smell? Did he wear cologne to bed or is that just his normal scent?*

I shook my head to focus. *What were we discussing? Oh yeah, my lovely nightmares.* "It's normal." I told him. "I went through a traumatic event, so it'll take some time."

"Less time if we get you some help. I hire military men for my security firm, Kayleigh. A number of them have had to deal with PTSD. I found a psychiatrist that specializes in PTSD and a particular therapy that is especially effective. It's called Eye

Movement Desensitization and Reprocessing therapy. Basically, you watch some lights in your peripheral vision and talk about your trauma."

"I have librarian insurance, Marc. There's no way it will cover that kind of specialized treatment." I dropped my gaze. I *hated* discussing things I couldn't afford.

He patted my thigh. "The psychiatrist works for me. It will cost you nothing. I'm not even going to blackmail you with the relationship agreement. I'm just going to help." He used his finger to tilt up my chin so my eyes met his. My mouth went dry, and I licked my lips. His gaze moved to them. "Don't fight me on this, Kayleigh. Please."

I ground my teeth. Torn between doing the right thing and my impulse to make my own choices, even if they were wrong. "Fine. I'll give it a try."

He nodded, slid off the bed, and turned to leave.

"Here, don't think you'll always get what you want." With that, I threw the signed agreement at him. He caught it, saw my signature on the agreement, and grinned.

I started seeing Marc's head shrinker the next day. I could not believe the change that it made in my life. Dr. Zoé made me call her by her first name, but I insisted on the Dr. part. Dr. Zoé was a miracle worker. One really doesn't understand how much trauma one has survived until you talk it out. Absent parents who turned everything over to my controlling uncle, my fights and capitulations to ensure my sister received the care she needed, and finally, after a hard-fought battle to get my sister's care in my hands, the attack that sent me to the hospital. She coaxed me into sharing the stress of urban car living, as I called it. We worked through everything.

$$6$$

Bourré

Marc

T hings were better now that Kayleigh was seeing Dr. Zoé. Kayleigh remained a colossal pain in my *tchu*, but at least the therapy was working. But with no rest for the weary, I now had another issue to solve. Armand, part of my Krewe, was going through a serious friction with his wife. That's why I called the rest of the Krewe to give him an intervention. Of course we did not call it that. We told him we were getting together to play *Bourré*. The whole Krewe came, even Etienne, who was on vacation from his FBI assignment in New Orleans. The Krewe of Roux was named after a Mardi Gras social group, and because we liked to cook, we added roux to our name as it's the base ingredient for making a gumbo.

Usually, a get together with the Krewe caused no issues, but that was BK, or before Kayleigh. Now Kayleigh deliberately misinterpreted the relationship agreement with the goal, often achieved, of annoying me. My lawyers wrote the agreement to protect Kayleigh. But equally and more importantly, they wrote the agreement so that Kayleigh would take all the holiday busy work off of my plate. Her job was to do the holiday activities that Sofia normally wanted to do with me. I hated telling my little goth, no, but the holidays were my busiest time of the year. With the uptick in home invasions and robberies and the need for personal protection for the holiday parties, I didn't have time to do everything my little munchkin wanted to do. My interpretation of the relationship agreement was that I had outsourced those activities to Kayleigh. But with Kayleigh, nothing was easy. Case in point, my interactions with her this afternoon. She waltzed into my study in a cloud of the lavender body spray I foolishly bought for her, an hour before my Bourré game with the Krewe.

She leaned over my antique mahogany desk, and I resisted the urge to lean towards her as she issued me orders. "Sofia's room in ten minutes. Be there."

I frowned over my glasses and blew out a breath. "Kayleigh, I'm busy. Can't you take care of it?"

She hopped on the corner of my desk, tipping over my green banker's lamp, and smirked. "Take care of signing your name on Christmas cards? That would be forgery, so no. You've been in this stupid office all day. Come spend some quality time with your daughter. Aren't you allotting precious time to play *Bourré* with your buddies tonight?"

My shoulders stiffened, and I glared at her. "That's to help a friend."

Unvexed, she countered, putting her face inches from mine. "And this is to help your daughter." She was infuriatingly correct. It didn't help that her proximity meant that I inhaled her lavender cinnamon scent.

On cue, my little goth walked in and broke the stalemate. Sofia dressed in black except for the pink tutu from dance class with her dark pig-tail braids curved up like Pippi Longstocking. "Hi, Daddy. Kayleigh and I have organized everything. We selected cards for everyone, we addressed the envelopes, I've even pre-signed the cards. As an added enticement —"

I glared at Kayleigh. That was not a ten-year-old's vocabulary. Sofia had clearly been coached. Kayleigh continued to lean back on my desk with her signature smirk.

My baby girl continued, but I knew I'd been beat. "—I made you your favorite peanut butter, oatmeal, and chocolate chip cookies. Ms. Kayleigh even made you some coffee, so you can be alert when you take some of your *valuable* time to play *Bourré* with your friends."

The biggest issue with Kayleigh was that she tag teamed me with Sofia. Outmanned and outgunned, I had no defenses against Sofia's particular brand of cute emotional blackmail. Tucking my glasses in my shirt pocket, I closed my report, and followed them out of the room. Ten minutes turned to an hour as I signed cards and read the funny ones that they had selected for our friends and family. When the doorbell rang, indicating my guests had arrived, I was chuckling over the Christmas card Sophia picked out for my friend Beau's family. It was a picture of children with Sharpie marker drawings on their faces and wished them a mischievous Christmas. I howled when I saw it because, not that long ago, Sofia had used Sharpie markers to give herself a goth makeover to resemble Abbie Sciutto from NCIS. Kayleigh tilted her head in curiosity.

"Later," I told her. "Just know that I hope the Babineaux *Littles* get inspired by our card."

"No problem. I'm sure Sofia will enlighten me. Enjoy your game. *Bonne chance.*" She and Sofia were whispering and tittering when I left the room. I glanced back, only to see Kayleigh's eyes trained on me, on my backside, to be specific. *Well, it's only fair. I look at hers often enough.*

Collecting my composure, I walked to the front hall and answered the door. I directed my friends to the game room where my staff had set up the *Bourré* table, snacks, and libations. My game room was our man cave, and the Krewe made themselves at home in there. The moment Armand arrived, I could tell he sensed an ambush. His eyebrows raised when I offered him a Swamp Pop rather than our usual LA31 beers.

"What's up? And what's with the coke?" he asked, raising up his Satsuma Fizz with a questioning look.

"Have a seat," I shuffled the deck, dealing everyone five cards, and turned over my last card. "Diamonds are trump. Who needs to change cards?"

Everyone except Armand exchanged cards. I guessed he had an excellent hand. What is that old saying about you can be either lucky in cards or love? I led with my king of hearts, which Armand smacked his ace on to the table and won the trick. He started the second trick with his nine of diamonds.

"Again, I ask," he said as he slapped down his card. "What's going on?"

We threw out our highest trump cards, the queen, the jack, the ten. Beau won the trick with his queen. He threw out an ace of clubs and hedged, "We just wanted to see how you were doing, you know, with the wedding planning."

Armand was skeptical. "*Ça c'est de la merde.*"

"*Merde* is a bad word," Sophia said from the doorway.

"It is, *Chérie*. What can we say instead?" I grinned and asked her.

"Ca ca in French and in English," she said.

"*C'est du caca,*" Armand corrected, while chuckling.

I walked over, picked Sophie up, and kissed her cheek. "Why aren't you in bed, sweetheart?"

She hugged me back. "I wanted to say goodnight to the Krewe and Ms. Kayleigh wants me to fetch her a Sarsaparilla Root Beer. You took all the Swamp Pops from the kitchen fridge."

Planting a soft kiss on her temple, I gave a soft pull on one of her braids. "Okay, darlin', but then it's to bed with you."

"*Oui, papa!*" She made the rounds, giving us each a hug goodnight. Then she dug in the cooler for an ice-cold

Sarsaparilla Root Beer, palming a Praline Cream Soda for herself, and scurried out of the game room. I just shook my head, familiar with her antics.

Etienne nodded, impressed with Sofia. "Smooth snaffle. I nearly missed the second coke that she palmed."

Beau focused instead on what Sof had said. He raised his eyebrow. "Kayleigh is still living here?"

My lips pressed together. I didn't lie to my Krewe, but this was not my secret to tell. "I couldn't drop her off at her apartment. Ahh ... it wasn't an option. Besides, she needed care, and it's safer here than ... where she was living. She's been through enough."

"But didn't she recover weeks ago?" Etienne, the *tchu,* was toying with me.

I narrowed my eyes at him. "She's safe and comfortable. Let it go."

"I will if you will," Armand mumbled, taking a gulp of his Satsuma Fizz. This brought us back to the point of this game, helping Armand.

Beau shook his head. "Not gonna happen until you explain why you're living in the barn instead of with your lovely fiancée, my cousin, and your two adorable children."

He explained about his night terrors and how he nearly hurt Renee. "I can't hurt her. Ever."

"Of course not. You're a protector," Etienne said. "Actually, you really are more like an Architect."

We all groaned. *Etienne and his pop psychology.* I rolled my eyes.

Etienne didn't pay us any mind. "What I mean is you need to protect others and you crave strategies and systems."

"I do like me a good system." Armand said, "But my VA shrink only offered drugs. I can't be hopped up at all times around my family."

I handed him Dr. Zoé's card. "Call this number."

Armand examined the card. "Who is it?"

"A psychiatrist that specializes in PTSD and a particular therapy that is especially effective. It's called, Eye Movement Desensitization Reprocessing. *Grosso Modo,* you watch some lights, especially in your peripheral vision, and you discuss what brought you to this point. Kayleigh hasn't had a nightmare in weeks since she started. I'm telling you, it's very effective."

"I can try it, but in the interim. I need to stay away from my family. They need to be safe." Then Armand set his ace and king down and won the pot. I happily threw my *Bourré* quarter into the pot. Now that we accomplished what we needed to, I was ready to enjoy the evening.

7

Helping Others

Kayleigh

Ms. Sue, Marc's mom, reached out the following day and asked if I wanted to spend time with her, Renee, and Renee's mom, Ms. Amelie. The library had become a refuge for me after the attack, and Ms. Sue, an ardent library supporter, had taken me under her wing. She considered the marriage license to be valid, and therefore, considered me to be family regardless of how often I reminded her that the marriage was temporary.

At that, Ms. Sue always brushed the back of her hand over my cheek and reminded me, "Everything is temporary, Kayleigh."

With a blink, I focused on the present. This would be my first social outing since before Stan attacked me. In preparation, I indulged in a bit of self-care, taking a warm shower using the cinnamon body wash Marc had left for me and spritzing myself with the lavender spray that I adored. I wondered, as I styled my now healthy blond waves in a high ponytail, how Marc knew to surround me with lavender and cinnamon. I asked his mama just that as I got into the SUV assigned to bring us to Renee's.

Ms. Sue shrugged. "He just told me to go shopping for you and said you liked those scents." *Weird.*

When we got to Renee's, my bodyguard scanned the perimeter and then made a beeline for the farmhand, Oscar. Like two peas in a pod, they discussed security/military stuff. I ignored them and climbed up the *Mes Rêves* porch. I loved *Mes Rêves*. Not only was it a beautiful two story Acadian house but also because Renee and Armand had transformed the entire property into a self-sufficient homestead. They had chickens, goats, vegetable gardens, and a fruit orchard. With on-site solar and wind power, they could go off-grid whenever they wanted. They hadn't made the jump yet, but it was only a matter of time.

As I walked up the porch stairs, Renee tilted her head and lifted her teacher's eyebrow. As a librarian, I recognized the expression. She was wondering what I was doing with a bodyguard. A bodyguard that she knew was on Marc's payroll.

"My guard." I said, rolling my eyes. "He follows me everywhere." I shrugged my shoulders, and we entered the house. Before the attack, the bric-à-brac and bright colors of *Mes Rêves* used to charm me. Now it put me on edge. *I can do this.* I followed Renee to the kitchen to prepare tea and snacks, while the mothers socialized in the living room.

"How're you feeling? I heard you'd woken up, but I thought you would be back in your new apartment by now. Why are you still at Marc's?" she asked, putting the water with tea bags and sugar to boil.

I flinched, and my eyes scanned the room, looking for a distraction. Marc had kept my secret, even from his best friends, for now. Pulling out the bread and sandwich fixins', I answered, "I'm at half-days at the library."

"Not my question, but I'll play along. Does your guard follow you to the library?" She asked, laying out all the bread.

I nodded, avoiding her gaze as I made the sandwiches. "It's a pain, but I've stopped fighting Mr. *Tête Dure* Richard about it. All he ever does is say that Sofia is worried about me. He guilts me into taking his help. Help that I don't need."

"Ah, that explains why you're still at his house. Other than hard-headed men, you doing okay?" She came over, cut the sandwiches, and arranged them on a serving tray.

I swallowed. "At first, I had terrible nightmares, reliving the attack every night. Lately, I've been sleeping better. The night terrors have stopped, for the most part."

Renee stilled. She did not take a breath. I glanced over at her. It was as if I could hear the gears turning in her mind.

Finally, she asked with a shaky voice, "How?"

"How what?" I opened a package of cookies and arranged them on a plate.

She grabbed my shoulder, her fingers twitched. "Kayleigh, how did you stop your nightmares?"

I turned and faced her and stared for a moment. She was flushed and fighting back tears; it dawned on me. "Armand?"

She nodded and then busied herself rearranging the cookie plate. "Yes, since his last mission. He moved to the barn. He won't come near me anymore. It's not an auspicious start to our real marriage." She rose, heading to the living room with the cookies.

I stopped her, gripping her forearm. "Stop. Let's talk. I have it too."

Renee stilled. "You have what?"

My eyes met hers. "PTSD, from stupid Stan. I barely remember the attack, but what I do recall gave me nightmares."

Taking a seat abruptly on the stool at the kitchen island, she buried her face in her hands. "What do I do?"

"I can't tell you what you need to do, but I can tell you what I do. Hold on a sec." I took out my phone, and texted Ms. Sue and Ms. Amelie, letting them know I needed time alone with Renee.

Ms. Amelie called from the living room. "We'll talk later, *Chérie!* We're taking the twins for a joy ride." After a moment, once they had rounded up the twins and their accoutrements, the front door slammed behind them.

Then I sat beside Renee, clasped both her hands in mine, and gave her the strategies that Dr. Zoé had given me. Together, we hatched a plan to get Armand back in the house, back in the wedding, and ready to celebrate Thanksgiving with his new family. We sent out a call for help that night.

The next morning, Renee's parents and Armand's mom, Ms. Rose, came to pick me up and head to Renee's farm. Marc was going with his Krewe later that morning, after he got Sofia settled with her *au pair*. When I walked to the SUV, Mr. Travis was driving, but both Ms. Amelie and Ms. Rose were in the back seat. Ms. Rose got out, and I took the seat between them. They each grabbed one of my hands and squeezed.

Ms. Rose spoke first. "Kayleigh, we don't know each other well. But you're my boy's cousin, so we're family. We just wanted you to understand how much we appreciate your help. You could've hidden your PTSD. A lot of people do. Instead, not only did you inform Renee that you had it, but you took the time to advise her on how she can support Armand. We just wanted to make sure that you comprehend what you've given them."

Tears welled in my eyes. They were such sweet, caring parents. I let a wave of emptiness pass before I answered them. "I really only gave her some pointers and ideas that helped me."

"You gave her hope. That was the best gift ever." Ms. Amelie gave me a kiss on one cheek while Ms. Rose kissed the other. I just basked in parental love all the way to *Mes Rêves.*

When we arrived, we started the morning in Renee's living room with coffee and planning. She doled out tasks to everyone. My job was to check that my suggestions, or rather Dr. Zoé's, were being implemented. These suggestions included adding lavender and rosemary house plants for their soothing aromas, incorporating ivy to purify the air, and including a tall ficus to foster tranquility and positivity. I ensured that they decluttered the house, especially at points of egress, so I, I mean Armand, didn't feel trapped in the house. I served as Renee's PTSD barometer. They went with my choice of paint color, which included a calming palette of white and pastel blue with pops of light green to bring joy. They even followed my suggestion to lighten the wood stain because the studies Dr. Zoé sent me said dark wood sparked feelings of sadness and disgust. Finally, we made a space for him with his own egress. Somewhere he could be calm. *Like my room and my secret garden entrance.*

After the home makeover, Renee pulled me to the side. We sat on her sofa in her newly decluttered living room. She waved and thanked everyone as they left, then she turned and hugged me. "You're my bestest friend, Kayleigh. But you went above and beyond. I've no idea what the outcome of tonight will be, but I do know, if we turn this around, it will be thanks to you."

"That's what friends are for, Renee." I hugged her back.

She held on tight and murmured, "Remember that next time you find yourself without a home."

I pulled away and glared. "Marc told you. That *fils d'putain*."

Renee scolded me. "First, don't talk about Ms. Sue that way or she won't serve us afternoon tea anymore, and second, Marc divulged nothing, but you just did. Don't try to con a teacher, Kayleigh. We have ways to make you talk. You think I haven't learned how to spot homeless kids? You told me you lost your apartment and then prevaricate when I mention your new apartment. I should have recognized the problem when I noticed your weight loss and food hoarding. Next time you get in a bind, promise me you will come to me."

My jaw clenched. "I promise. Doesn't matter, anyway. I'm staying with Marc for now, through the holidays."

"Just through the holidays, huh?" Renee hugged me again and laughed. "Well, have fun with that. It's not all about doing for others, you realize. You can't take care of others if you don't take care of yourself. Frolic a bit."

My stomach clenched as I tried to breathe, frolicking did not sound responsible. *Maybe a little fun with Sofia. I could do that.*

8

Planning and Plotting

Kayleigh

My holiday *fun* started the next morning in Marc's fancy modern kitchen. Sofia and I were preparing for the upcoming Thanksgiving feast. In the spirit of *carpe diem,* we resolved to start with desserts first. As such, Sofia had texted out a question to the entire Krewe.

She and I enjoyed our morning hot chocolates. Sofia's included added peppermint and a candy cane to stir with. Mine had cinnamon and cayenne, a recipe that my friend Renee's Mawmaw had taught us. While we savored the chocolate, we pulled out all the normal ingredients to make a cookie base recipe as we waited for responses. As we mixed the dry ingredients, the responses came in rapid fire. Shell texted about her family.

> Shell: Beau and Tanner love chocolate chips, plain or peanut butter, whatever you want to bake. Val likes ginger snaps and Bailey Marie wants sugar cookies with pastel sprinkles.

Later in the day Renee wrote to us.

> Renee: Three votes for Sofia's famous peanut butter, oatmeal, and chocolate chip cookies for me and the twins. Armand wants molasses cookies.

Gelly was the last person to text.

> Gelly: Etienne was going to vote with me for Sofia's famous cookies, but then he saw Armand's selection and the traitor has jumped ship for the molasses cookies.

We made them all. Sofia was a whirling dervish in the kitchen. Chef Agnès stayed away but emphasized that we would need to clean up after ourselves if we wanted breakfast the next day. As Sofia pulled a tray of molasses cookies out of the oven and I placed them on the cooling rack, she asked me, "Since you and Daddy got married, can I call you Mama now?" Sofia measured out more flour, oatmeal, and baking powder.

"Your daddy married me to keep me safe." Sofia nodded at that. That jibed with her view of her father. I found some more big mixing bowls and pulled those out as well.

Sofia started measuring sugar and eggs in a bowl and microwaved some butter in another so she could add it to the mixture. "So, I can call you Mama now? I never got to call anyone Mama."

I watched as she measured out pecans and chocolate chips. She tried averting her eyes, but they kept flashing me a wistful look. "Ah ... that might not be a good idea. You never met your mother?"

She pulled out the butter, adding it to the bowl with sugar and eggs. Once that was smooth, she added those wet ingredients to the dry ingredients in the flour bowl. She kept her voice level and focused on her task when she answered. "My real mama didn't want me. I heard Daddy talking. He had to pay her to keep me. Can I tell you a secret?" Sofia whispered, handing me the chocolate chips and crushed pecans to mix into the batter. This kid was a whiz in the kitchen.

"Only in the secret garden," I told her. Thinking of the device Marc had used to check the rooms. If it wasn't safe for his secrets in the house, I didn't want Sofia divulging hers. She nodded.

"As for calling me mama. While I would love to be your mama, it might be too early for that. Your daddy married me to protect me. It is a temporary marriage to keep me safe from danger. That danger won't be there forever. He's probably going to want to marry someone he loves, not just someone he's trying to protect." For some reason, that thought annoyed me.

Sofia nodded at that because that was what her daddy did. She blended all the ingredients until they were as smooth as possible. Then she added some more chocolate chips.

Time to change the subject. "I have, however, agreed to stay for the holidays. So, let's talk holiday activities. What all do you want to do this holiday season?"

"Anything?" She formed cookie balls and put them on pans.

"Anything." I arranged the dirty bowls and mixer in the sink with care. While Chef Agnès wanted the kitchen cleaned, that responsibility was on Sofia's shoulders. Agnès had banned me from washing dishes after an accidental incident with a crystal pitcher. An *antique* crystal pitcher. At any rate, Chef Agnès fed me and fed me well, so I would not be crossing her.

I turned to see Sofia behind the kitchen island with some milk and some cookies from yesterday. "Well, I want all my honorary cousins for Thanksgiving. I'm officially a Little, you know." She dunked her cookie in her milk and took a big bite.

"They'll be there. The entire Krewe will be there. We also have the menu that we worked on. What about after that?"

"I want to try the crazy Black Friday shopping. Bailey Marie went with her parents last year and then they lost her. When she asked for help, the cashiers ignored her. So, she had to stand on a counter until security came. That sounded like fun."

With my eyes closed, I imagined the *fun*. "Uh ... from an adult perspective, that sounds like a nightmare."

"Bailey Marie did say her mama wouldn't stop hugging her. But that sounded like fun as well."

Poor Shell, that must've been horrifying. "Well, I'll talk to your daddy about it. But I'm pretty sure he knows about the Bailey Marie incident, and if that happened to my cousin, you'll be shopping with an entire security force around you."

Sofia sighed, "I know." She got up from her chair when the oven dinged and slid her pans into the pre-heated oven.

"Where's the paper in this kitchen?" I asked. She pointed to a drawer, and I pulled out a notebook. I wrote on the top of the page, *Our Holiday Plans,* and then asked, "Ok, let's get all of our plans down in black and white. I have Thanksgiving with the Babineaux with our splendiferous menu of Turducken; dirty rice, pecan pie, green bean casserole, sweet potato casserole, and all the cookies we can make. Was there anything you wanted to add?"

Sofia thought for a minute. "Mawmaw Babineaux's blueberry and banana pie?"

I added it to the list. "Mmm. That's one of my favorites. Now, what other activities do you want to do?"

She came up with a list, and I wrote it all down. As per Marc's request, I tried to direct the list to include only events in the area, so that security would not become an issue. For each event, we also included what I called the *Prix Gourmande,* which would be the fun and tasty prize we would eat or drink during the celebration. The list included the following:

1. Thanksgiving with family with a menu of Turducken; dirty rice, pecan pie, green bean casserole, sweet potato casserole, and Mawmaw Babineaux's blueberry and banana pie.

2. Black Friday shopping. Sofia promises not to wander off. *Prix Gourmande:* Hot Chocolate or Pumpkin Spice Lattes from Black Café.

3. Noël au Village at Acadian Village. *Prix Gourmande:* Hot chocolate, even if it's not cold.

4. Decorate the house for Christmas. *Prix Gourmande:* Christmas cookies and milk for Sofia and *Vin Chaud* for Kayleigh (Chef Agnès said she makes a mean *Vin Chaud*)

5. *Danse avec moi* Christmas Recital. *Prix Gourmande:* Myran's malts and milkshakes after the recital.

6. *Christmas on the Bayou boat parade. Prix Gourmande:* Meat pies and sweet potato pies.

7. Cajun Night Before Christmas party. *Prix Gourmande:* Chex Mix.

8. Christmas at home in PJs. *Prix Gourmande:* Chef Agnès' famous crêpes.

9. Change decorations from Christmas to Epiphany and *Mardi Gras season. Prix Gourmande:* Keller's Cream

Cheese filled King Cake.

> 10. Make our own king cake (but have an emergency
>   Keller cream cheese filled one just in case)

"Whad'ya think?" I asked her, while trying to figure out how we would get all of these activities completed in a little over a month.

"A holiday adventure! A delicious holiday adventure! I'm showing Daddy." Sofia ran to find her dad so she could show him our list. When she returned, she was smiling because Marc had approved every single activity. Of course he had. He wasn't organizing them. Shaking off my annoyance, I greeted Sofia with a smile. Then I got straight to work on developing a detailed schedule. As a librarian, I fully understood the necessity of logistics when juggling numerous activities involving children.

"When can we start?" Sofia asked, peering around my shoulder at our calendar of events.

"We start with Thanksgiving with the Krewe and all you Littles." I tugged one of her braids. "Is your room ready for guests?"

She ran from the kitchen with a, "It will be."

The corner of my mouth quirked up when I realized she had left me to save all the cookies. I put each type of cookie in a separate container. Of course, I took a sample of each one first. Perks of the job. *I'm counting this as frolicking.* I dunked my last cookie in milk and headed to my room to rest.

9

Thanksgiving Meeting

Marc

I met with the entire Krewe of Roux — myself, Beau, Etienne, and Armand, in my new safe room. Well, more like my Armageddon-safe luxury studio apartment. *What can I say? Safety First. Safety Always.* I enjoy nice things and I worry about security. It was past time we dealt with the attacks we'd been defending against for years. The latest being the attack on Kayleigh. No more playing defense.

So far, we had pieced together some clues. We knew that it was Kayleigh's Nonc Bill Breaux behind the attacks. We knew the attacks were linked to an inheritance, and the only ones targeted, aside from Kayleigh, were Bill's illegitimate children. Also, we had a rusty old key that Etienne found, which we hypothesized might be for a safe deposit box. Those were our only clues.

"Any news on the key?" Etienne asked.

"My PI has been working on it. He's meeting us here today for an update." I told them.

"While I reckon this is the fanciest panic room I've ever seen, why are we meeting in here?" Beau asked.

"I found some bugs in Kayleigh's room and in my study."

"Told ya. You have a mole." Armand said.

"Yes, I'm aware, and I believe it's Paul. I looked into everyone's financial and phone records."

"Paul was dumb enough to call Billy boy on his phone?" Armand asked.

"Only once. Then there is a distinct hole when he doesn't call anyone once a week. I had him followed by my PI agency and he's met with Mr. Breaux twice since Kayleigh got injured. Plus, he has a hidden account with quite a chunk of change in it."

"Why haven't you fired the *tchu*, then?" Beau asked. His body shaking with frustration. Bill Breaux had ordered attacks on Beau's kids three times already. While each attack had been thwarted, it was time to put a stop to it.

"Because I want to use him to feed Billy boy some misinformation." I told them. "You're familiar with the saying. Keep your friends close, but your enemies closer?"

On the video feed, we saw Kayleigh and Sofia making cookies and giggling together. The abrasive, rabid bunny was nowhere in sight. Instead, Kayleigh was sunshine and rainbows, beaming at my daughter.

"Are they safe in the interim?" Etienne asked. As an FBI agent, security was always on his brain.

"Yes, I have my most trusted people on them 24/7. And before you ask, yes, I've recently re-screened all my staff. I believe Paul is the lone traitor."

The front door screen showed an older man buzzing the doorbell. I hit my intercom button and said, "Welcome, Joe. C'mon in." Inside the foyer, we could see Paul question Joe. I hit the intercom for that area and said, "Send him to my safe room, Paul."

Paul followed him to the room.

"He may be a rat, but he senses something is going down," Armand said.

When the PI arrived at my safe room, I exchanged a brief thank you with Paul before swiftly closing the door in his face. I ushered Joe into the room and we watched as Paul checked on his fellow security team and then walked out to the far edges of the property. Assuming he was out of the range of the security system.

He dialed on a burner flip phone. "I'm sure they're on to me … no, I'm of no use to you … no, don't hurt him. I'll stay in … alright, but I'm saying I don't expect you can trust the intel I get you from here on out. No, I wouldn't trust her phone either. I'm pretty sure the boss put a tracer and listening device on it. I don't think he has given it back to her. He wants her to focus on recovery. Yeah, I'll let you know when she leaves the property."

"Smart treasonous bastard," Beau said.

"Smart, but with a weakness," Joe added.

"Any idea what that weakness is?" I asked him.

"Same one that your new wife has," Joe answered. Everyone froze at that statement.

"What weakness is that?" Etienne asked.

Joe responded, "Mr. Breaux bought the Happy Place assisted living home about six months ago. Insurance, as you know, doesn't cover that kind of specialized care and insured people can rarely get their siblings or grandparents covered. He raised the rates, but offered some special deals, to Paul's grandfather and to Ms. Kayleigh's sister for a brief period, but those rates inflated each month. Until this month, when Kayleigh's sister's rates went away."

I nodded. "Because of my threatened lawsuit. "

Armand asked. "Who does Kayleigh have in a nursing home?"

I answered, "Her sister, Claire. She was hit by a drunk driver and has been in the home since. Actually, they were both hit by what they thought was a drunk driver, but after all that has happened, I'm starting to doubt that story. The driver was never found. Anyway, Claire was moved from the ICU to the Happy Place assisted living home."

Armand scratched his head. "So that's how Bill forced Kayleigh to date Stan?"

All eyes turned to Etienne, waiting for his response. "Yep, I was there when the Sheriff, Bradley, interviewed Stan. Stan admitted to threatening Claire, anytime Kayleigh wouldn't do what he wanted."

Armand paced the room, muttering, "I'm her cousin. I should have realized this."

Meanwhile, my voice quieted. "What do you mean, what he wanted, Etienne?"

Etienne held up his hands. "Oh, not that. Breaux is a firm believer in no sex before marriage."

Beau scoffed at that, "Armand and my eldest children resulted from his extra-marital affairs. "

Etienne shrugged. "I meant for women, not men." We shook our heads at that idiocy.

I spoke to Joe. "Keep your eyes on that home for me. I'm getting Claire out as soon as I've made the house accessible to her. That should be soon. Find out what we need to do to get Paul's grandfather out of there as well. Does Bill own it outright or just controlling interest?"

Joe rifled through his notes. "He owns 33 percent and the rest of the owners have much smaller shares. So, he made himself the director."

I nodded. "Buy me what you can. Quietly. Now, tell us what you found out about the key."

Joe brightened. "You were right. It's a safe deposit box key. After many attempts, we located the bank and the box." He pulled out some ancient papers from his beat-up briefcase.

Looking them over, I took out my phone and called Beau's lawyer cousin on speaker. "Kevin, we need some legal advice. It's about the attacks on the *Littles* and your new brother-in-law."

"For the *Littles*, I can be there in ten minutes," Kevin said.

"Hey, what about me?" Armand groused.

"For my sister's husband, I'll meet you after lunch."

Chuckling, I added, "There's one hiccough. How's your French? The documents look to be in what I would guess is eighteenth century French."

"Then I'll ask my boss, Mr. Trahan, to come along. He loves to collect those old French legal contracts. Expect him to make you an offer when he arrives."

"If he can help us protect the Littles, he can have them as a Christmas present," I told him.

"In that case, you can be sure Hercule will drop everything and head over there."

"Kevin, say nothing, especially once you get to the house. We're having a bit of a mole infestation." I watched Paul on the video monitors, pretending to be protecting us. Even knowing that he was being blackmailed did not stem my rage.

"Understood. We'll see you soon."

When Kevin hung up, we lingered in the calm of my safe room for another hour before we joined everyone in the chaotic Thanksgiving festivities. Kayleigh and Sof had gone all out on the decorations. Turkeys made of hand outlines adorned every surface, adding a festive touch. Hand-drawn turkeys and cornucopias embellished the place-cards on both the adult and children's tables. Instrumental Christmas music played in the background as the adults chatted and ate what my Chef Agnès called *amuse-bouches*. I couldn't figure out what was in them, but they were divine. While we noshed, chatted, and tried to ignore the looming danger, Sofia had gathered the rest of the *Littles* in the living room to watch *A Charlie Brown Thanksgiving*. At last, the moment arrived for us to feast on the mouthwatering Thanksgiving meal Kayleigh and Sofia had planned.

The adults' table for the Thanksgiving festivities was more subdued as the Krewe and I processed what we had learned earlier. I sent the traitorous Paul home for Thanksgiving to avoid any potential mischief he might stir up. The youngest *Littles* ate in the kitchen with their grandparents, who wanted alone time with the babies. This provided the adults with a much-needed opportunity to unwind. The older *Littles* were with my parents at the older kids' table. Since Sofia was their only grandchild, they enjoyed spending that time with her.

Kayleigh started the meal with a Thanksgiving prayer, "Thank you for our friends, our children, and our family (at least the good family)." Everyone chuckled. "Thank you for this food, and may the world be a happier and more peaceful place. Amen."

After that, I sliced the Turducken and distributed a platter of sliced meat to each table. Once the children were served, we began our meal and passed the food around the tables, discussing the upcoming holidays. Post-meal, the Krewe and I gathered around the TV, savoring the sight of the Saints crushing the Ravens. All the while, we digested our Thanksgiving meal and incubated strategies to protect everyone.

10

Thanksgiving & Black Friday

Kayleigh

The next week was a whirlwind. After the wedding that almost wasn't, it warmed my heart to see how happy my friend Renee was with Armand, knowing that sharing my experiences with PTSD and therapy had played a role in her contentment. Marc, in turn, had convinced Armand to consult my therapist, and now Renee and her fam navigated bumps in their path with skill. Today, everyone was coming over for our Thanksgiving feast.

Sofia had started with Chef Agnès in the kitchen. They worked together on the menu that we had included on the fridge. In addition, Chef Agnès wanted to make a variety of *amuse-bouches* and football food since the Krewe would be watching the Saints play the hated Ravens today as the Thanksgiving game. Sofia was in an adorable apron.

"Here you go ma ... Ms. Kayleigh." She kept doing that lately. Each time she nearly said mama, my heart broke a little more. Even before I moved in with Marc for this sham of a marriage,

I adored my little Sofia. She was a reader extraordinaire at the library, and this bled into our daily interactions as we often just sat in Marc's study and read together silently. We were kindred spirits. The urge to hug her and not let go was strong. If my life were less complicated, maybe ...

She watched me for a few minutes. Afterwards, she whispered in my ear. "Can I tell you my secret now?" She'd been asking every hour on the hour and I'd been putting her off. Not sure if I wanted to learn her secret.

"Yes, let me find a stopping point and we can head to the garden for Thanksgiving crafts. While I'm doing that, can you make me some more coffee? I have a feeling I'll be needing it. Chef Agnès, would you like a cup?" Sofia put another pod in the coffee maker when mine had finished. After, she threw the pods into the recycling bin. She handed me and Chef Agnès our coffees.

"You're a sweet girl, Ms. Kayleigh. A terrible cook, but a sweet girl. Not like the fine chef you will be, Sofia *ma chérie,*" Agnès said.

Sofia had put together a green bean casserole as I finished up my list of lists. She kissed Agnès' cheek as I got up.

"You ready, my little book dragon?" I had started calling her a book dragon when I accidentally entered her closet and discovered her hoard of books. The majority of which were overdue library books that Marc had simply paid for.

"Yes." Sofia giggled and washed her hands, and slid the green bean casserole she had assembled to Chef Agnès.

We gathered the materials we needed to make the Thanksgiving decorations and entered the secret garden through my room. I deposited the crafting supplies in the folly and told her we should walk and talk. After Marc found those bugs, I wanted to ensure that if a bug listened to our conversation, the listeners would only catch whispers of Sofia's hidden secret. They wouldn't hear her actual secret.

"So, hit me with it, Sofia. What did you want to tell me?"

Sofia put her hand in mine and squeezed. "Daddy takes care of everyone. I know because he kept me."

I squeezed her hand back. "Well, of course, sweetie. You're his daughter and he loves you."

Sofia shook her head. "That's my secret. I was listening once when he was in his study. There's a closet near Daddy's study where you can hear everything in there. Anyway, he was talking to Mawmaw Sue. She told him that he was such an angel for raising some other man's child. He got really mad at her."

I shrugged my shoulders. "So you're adopted."

"My mom tricked him. She made him think I was his, but then something about my blood type showed him I wasn't his. So I wanted you to know that my daddy will take care of you forever. You don't have to worry, because he's going to take care of me forever and I'm not even his daughter." A tear slipped over her cheek.

Stepping in front of her, I used my fingers to tip her face up to look me in the eye. "Sofia Charlene Richard. You take that back. Aren't you an honorary Little?"

A soft smile creased her lips. "Yes. Bailey Marie is my bestest friend."

"And who are the Little's parents?"

"Mr. Beau and Ms. Shell."

With a hand, I tucked a stray dark lock behind her ear. "Would you consider Bailey Marie as their daughter?"

"Of course, they'd do anything for her. Daddy told me she has them wrapped around her little finger. She just says mama or daddy and they give her everything she wants."

I cupped her cheek as I reasoned, "So if Bailey Marie, Valerie, and Tanner can be adopted and belong to the family, why can't you? I think your daddy adores you. No, I'm certain your daddy adores you."

Sofia gazed at her feet and shook her head. "But he is mad at my mommy. Maybe one day I'll do something wrong and he won't love me anymore."

Again, I tipped us her chin as I tilted my head in inquiry. "I'm sorry, who has a hoard of overdue library books that her daddy just pays for because his little book dragon doesn't want to give up any of her hoard?"

She laughed at that. "Me, I'm the Book Dragon."

"You are indeed." I hugged her to me. "And you have your daddy wrapped around your little finger as well. Go ahead and tell him that you want that new silver sparkly tutu for your dance recital. I bet he'll get it express mailed. Ask him to read the Secret Garden to you again, for the hundredth time. I bet he will in a heartbeat, because you are his little girl."

"I love you, Ms. Kayleigh." She hugged me.

"And I love you, my little book dragon. Now, let's get these decorations made and you can let me know what you want me to burn for the Thanksgiving feast today?"

After the Thanksgiving feast, in which I worked as a sous-chef under Agnès and burned nothing, the time had come for Black Friday shopping. We gathered in the kitchen early Friday morning. We considered heading out right after the festivities, but it felt mean to make workers miss the entire holiday because we wanted good deals.

As I warned Sofia, we had an entourage of security around us. As if we were rock stars. Clueless people even took pictures thinking we were someone important and not just the wards of an overprotective OCD security freak.

"Do *not*, under any circumstances, let go of my hand," I told Sofia.

"Yes, Ms. Kayleigh. Safety First. Safety Always," she repeated her dad's security firm motto.

While others flocked to big box stores and mega marts for deals, we headed to bookstores where a book dragon and a librarian could find reading materials and warm beverages.

"Doesn't look to be too many people here," the bodyguard named Steven told us.

I scanned the bookstore and, to my chagrin, spotted Marlene Breaux, my Nonc Bill's wife. "What's she doing here?" I asked. Tante Marlene was Nonc Bill's trophy wife and minion. If she was here, it was at his behest. A reader she was not.

Steven and the rest of the protection entourage went into lockdown mode. While they took pictures of her, they kept us in the SUV.

"Let's head to the next location, and you can shop here once we don't have any sketchy characters about," one bodyguard said.

"Whose that?" Sofia asked.

"Marlene, Nonc Bill's wife."

"The uncle that tried to hurt you?"

I cocked my head to the side. *How did she figure that out?*

Sofia leaned toward me and whispered, "The closet next to the study."

I must warn Marc about that closet.

"Yes. I don't trust her. No problem, I love the little independent *Beausoleil* bookstore. If I ever get my dream bookstore, I want it to be like that one," I told our entourage.

Sofia smiled. "It's one of my favorites, but they don't have a coffee shop, so no coffee and book reading for you and no hot chocolate and books for me."

Shrugging my shoulders, I said, "Black Café is right near there. Let's get our beverages from them and then head to the bookstore."

We purchased our drinks and afterwards headed into *Beausoleil Books*, surrounded by security.

A sales lady walked up to us. "How can I help you ladies?"

"Children's classics for me. Some *Magic Treehouse*, and *Junie B Jones* for my book dragon over there. After that, we want to just buy some books and curl up in your seating area and read them. Can we drink our cocoa and coffee in here?" I asked her.

"Absolutely, but you know the rule with drinks." She handed us each an adorable woven basket.

I grinned. "You break it, you buy it. I'm aware. I'm a librarian in Breaux Bridge."

"Well, it's a pleasure to meet you. Enjoy. I'm putting some Christmas music on. Any requests?"

"See, this is why I love independent bookstores. How about *Creole Christmas?* Do you have that album?" I asked.

"*Bien sûr*! I'll play it for you. Which song do you want to listen to?"

I grinned. "I love 'Let It Snow' by Rockin' Dopsie and the Zydeco Twisters."

She nodded. "Excellent selection. Enjoy your time and let me know when I can check you out." She walked away and "Let It Snow" started playing through the bookstore sound system.

We rifled through the shelves, putting books in our little baskets. With our book purchases complete, we sat in the Beausoleil reading nook and devoured our new book hoard. At times, I'd laugh and read a passage to Sofia. At other times, she'd read a passage back to me from her book. After an hour, the bell above the door chimed. We glanced up to see my harried aunt, Marlene Breaux. I got up and stepped in front of Sofia. This alerted the security team, and they blocked her access to me.

"I'm her aunt and must speak with her. Now!" I shook my head, and the guard did not budge.

"If you want your sister alive, you'll listen to what I have to say."

I glared at her. "Don't threaten my sister. I'll listen to you from there, but don't you dare threaten Claire. Say your piece."

"Alone," she ordered, expecting to be obeyed.

"I'm sorry. The last time I was alone with someone in your family, I was put in a coma. Tell me what you have to say, so you can leave." I kept Sofia in place behind me.

My aunt muttered, "I'm surprised you haven't learned your lesson."

"Say. What. You. Must. Then. Leave!"

"Bill wants to meet with you. At the assisted living home, be there this coming Monday or your sister will be thrown on the street."

"That's illegal and the Happy Place is already courting a lawsuit when it comes to my sister."

She laughed at that. "It's funny that you think that matters. Be there or else."

"You've delivered your message. Now get out."

Following her departure, I struggled to maintain a cheerful demeanor, but my interest in shopping had faded.

Sofia fake yawned. "I think I want to go home now."

"I'm sorry I ruined our day."

"You didn't. I have plenty of new books to add to my hoard and presents for nearly everyone."

When we got back, she ran to her room, and I snuck to mine. Exhausted, I fell into the bed. I didn't see a way out. I'd give Sofia one last weekend of fun and then I'd have to figure out a way to get myself and my sister out of this fiasco alive.

11

Inheritance Mystery

Marc

I didn't join Kayleigh and Sofia on their Black Friday shopping spree, as I preferred to delegate those tasks to my well-compensated team. While I was doing my daily work, I could watch the footage of their excursion from the comfort of my private safe room. The footage captured a mix of in-house Thanksgiving activities and their adventures outside the compound.

Watching Sofia as she admitted to knowing she was not my biological child, I nearly swallowed my tongue. My little goth was too observant. Going forward, I'd need to be on my toes to keep secrets from Sofia. The fact that the bitch, Tracy, pretended she was mine did not matter to me. Even after I knew the truth, I had already held Sofia in my arms. The first time I cradled her with her shock of black hair and her red face crying, my heart melted. When she wrapped her tiny fist around my finger, I was hooked. She became forever my little girl. I was grateful that Kayleigh eased her worries. *Sofia needs someone like Kayleigh for a mama.*

I kept having to remind myself that Kayleigh was a pain in my *tchu*. It didn't work. I pulled my fingers through my hair. The rabid little bunny was growing on me. In my mind, she had transformed into a snarky Tinker Bell. That metaphor was more apt. I'd always had a thing for Tinker Bell, and this one came with a plush rosebud mouth. Like Tink, everything she did, she did to protect people she held dear. Usually children, because no one had protected her. I shook my head and focused on the video feed.

The bookstore footage enraged me. Mr. Breaux was relentless, adept at achieving his goals without tarnishing his own hands. But using his own wife to threaten Kayleigh gave him a whiff of desperation. I needed to know why, so I texted Hercule and Kevin to see if they had an update on deciphering those ancient French legal documents we discovered.

> Any progress on those documents? Mr. Breaux just sent his wife to tell Kayleigh they'd throw her sister in the street if she didn't meet with him in two days. I need information ASAP.

> Hercule: Yes, Mr. Richard. We have gotten them translated by a certified and highly prestigious translator with expertise in 18th century French to ensure that its authenticity would be unquestionable.

> Kevin: We also verified that everything was filed with the proper authorities and included the authenticated seal of the local magistrate. I'm printing the translation as we speak.

While I waited, I studied the video more closely. Something in Kayleigh's expression conveyed a mixture of sadness and apprehension. She appeared, for lack of a better word, hunted. I thought about her living in her car. She'd suffer to ensure that Claire remained protected. If she felt Sofia was also in danger, she'd suffer more. My chest rose and fell with a sigh. Sofia had tried to convince her I would always help her. From her facial expression, Kayleigh did not believe her and was preparing to bear the weight of all familial responsibilities yet again. I needed to convince her I wasn't like the rest of her family. A sudden realization grabbed me by the throat. I considered Kayleigh to be part of my family. A family that I needed to protect.

Within a half hour, Kevin came over in a business suit paired with his dress cowboy boots. It was still hard to get used to seeing my old high school buddy like that. Mr. Trahan was as he always was, dapper and elegant. He strode into my house in his bow tie, designer suit, and handmade loafers. I grew up with his son, Sheriff Bradley Trahan, and besides their love for justice and the law, they were diametric opposites. Bradley was country, with a capital C, with cowboy hats and boots and a 'well shucks' kind of easy charm. That charm diffused many issues in our parish and made us all safer. Hercule personified class and elegance, the Atticus Finch of Meauxville. A soft-spoken man that wielded the law like a big stick. If he wanted an in-person meeting, it was to discuss something important.

I met them both at the door and walked them to my study. With manners drilled into me by my mother, I asked them. "How are you both doing? Can I offer either of you a cup of coffee?"

"No time for chitchat, young man," Hercule told me and snapped his fingers. "Kevin, the translations, please."

Kevin pressed his lips together, more amused than annoyed at his boss's heavy-handed methods. He reached into his briefcase and pulled out a binder. He set the binder on the desk in front of me. "On the left-hand side is the original French. On the right is the translated text. We have marked the most pertinent pages with post-its."

Hercule cleared his throat, and I reached into my mini-fridge and pulled out a Perrier for him. "Thank you, Marc." He drank some water, wiped off his hands with a clean handkerchief, and pulled a notebook from his blazer. "Please turn to the section marked with the number one."

I flipped the binder to the post-it with a one on it.

Hercule pointed to the French section. "According to this provision in the will, the heirs must consent to the condition that any descendants, whether legitimate or not, are entitled to a portion of the monetary and property assets."

Kevin flipped to the last section of the binder. "I found a legal agreement that Breaux and Kayleigh's father, Carl, signed to that extent."

I frowned. "So, Kayleigh's parents should have gotten half the funds since her father is Bill's brother. Why is she struggling for funds, and why are they trying to marry her off?"

Hercule turned the page in the binder. "This might help to explain it." He showed us another document. "When he was eighteen, Kaleigh's daddy signed a document turning all management of the funds over to Bill. I'll research the first matter. Based on the initial document, her father should have gotten funds, and, legally, he should not have been able to turn them over to William, according to the provisions of the will. As for the last matter, Bill's probably found a lackey who agreed to a pre-nuptial agreement that would give the lackey funds in exchange for Kayleigh relinquishing her money to Bill. The cad."

With a guilty grimace, I turned to Kevin. "I have a pre, or rather, post-nuptial agreement with Kayleigh."

Hercule cleared his throat. "About that, you will need to send it to me. I'll have to add her inheritance once we figure out what that is. She needs to sign it with full knowledge of what she has. I need to protect her interests."

"Understood." I nodded to Hercule. "Can you leave this binder with me? I'd like to examine it in detail. Also, Kevin has a copy of our relationship agreement. Look it over based on this new information and make whatever changes you deem necessary to protect Kayleigh's interest. I can promise to sign it. We might not get along, but I'll always protect Kayleigh. With that being said, I can't guarantee that Kayleigh will agree to the new document. It took some convincing to get her to sign the first one."

Kevin picked up his sleek, leather briefcase and headed towards the door. "I'll make those changes and send them over in a half hour."

I shook my head. "Why don't you both meet us at Acadian Village? We're having a family gathering there. You can talk to the whole Krewe and have some fun while you're at it."

Based on the new information, I strengthened the security detail at Acadian Village. I'd already rented out the entire village to avoid any pushback from the management. In addition, because Claire was also an heir, I sent security to the Happy

Place assisted living facility. I needed to ensure Claire's safety while she was still at the home, in case Mr. Breaux acted on the threat issued through his wife. Besides, she was family and not just Kayleigh's responsibility now. My list of people to protect was growing alarmingly long.

12

Noël au Village

Kayleigh

Tonight, we were all going together to *Noël au Village* in Acadian Village. Sofia was bouncing up and down in her red and green plaid leggings and her black velvet tunic. She even had matching velvet ear warmers and a black cloche. Compared to her, I was vastly underdressed. I was in my favorite Christmas message tee with a santa hat, blue jeans, and bells that attached to my ankle boots. My t-shirt read *Santa, before I explain, how much do you know?* Sofia tilted her head back and forth as she read, trying to understand. Marc, in contrast, snorted and started coughing when he saw the shirt. Marc was much more posh than I, in his fancy western shirt stretched across his chest, ironed blue jeans that fit him well, and expensive ostrich cowboy boots. The only non-cowboy element were those adorable wire-rimmed glasses that gave him an air of an engineer.

I rolled my eyes at him and called to Sofia. "We're meeting your honorary cousins, and my actual cousins, there!"

Beau and Shell Babineaux were meeting us there with their children, *The Littles,* as we affectionately called them. We included Sofia as a *Little* as well. Basically, any child related to the Krewe of Roux, were considered Littles. That was perhaps a sexist definition, but I was letting things go at this point. I mean, while Shell, Renee, Gelly, and I were friends, we did not name our group, nor did we climb treehouses and put 'No boys allowed signs' on the door. Whatever, today was about lights, hot chocolate, and dancing to Cajun music.

"If we have the same cousins, then are we related?" Sofia asked, pulling my thoughts back to her.

I walked over and set her hat at a jaunty angle. "Well, I'm a Breaux, and you're a Richard. Somewhere, I'm sure, our family trees no doubt cross. How about next time we're in the library, we head to the genealogy section. We can each make a family tree and find out if and how we're related."

"Libraries are the best, aren't they?" she sighed.

I grinned. "That they are, my little book dragon. That they are. Ready for lights, dancing, and hot chocolate?" Brushing back a lock of Sofia's dark hair that had escaped her cloche, I kissed her forehead.

She hugged me. "*Bien sûr.* I can't wait to drink *chocolat chaud.*"

We both climbed into one of Marc's huge black SUVs and headed to our destination. Marc was inside texting on his phone. He looked up, smiled at Sofia, and opened his arm so she could snuggle up next to him. I tilted my head as I reflected on the fact that Sofia's hair color was an exact match to Marc's, which was odd based on what she told me. To tell the truth, she gave every appearance of being his biological daughter. I wondered if Sofia was wrong or if she had misunderstood what she overheard.

When we arrived at Acadian Village, I scanned the parking lot. "Why are there only big black SUVs?" I asked Marc.

"It's a popular vehicle?" Marc hedged, nodding to a text on his phone and then asking the driver to open the door to let us out.

Sofia got out and waved to her cousins, who were heading to the entrance. At the gate, the usual greeter from LARC, the organization that used *Noël au Village* to raise money for adults with special needs, was missing. In its place was Marc's security team.

I turned to him and raised my eyebrow. "So, you rented out the entire *Noël au Village*?"

"What? It's easier to keep everyone safe, and it's for a good cause." Marc said, nodding to our bodyguards to follow us in. I noticed that Beau and Shell's family, and Armand and Renee and the twins, had a protective detail as well.

"Not overboard at all," I muttered to myself.

"No, it's not. Safety first. Safety always. Let's get y'all into the village."

A man in a three-piece suit came out to meet us. The guards stepped in front of him.

"I'm Mr. Smith, the director of LARC. I just wanted to thank you for your donation to our organization. Because of you, our clients will be able to live, work, and be independent."

"You do good work, Mr. Smith. We have the village to ourselves, except for the performers and vetted workers, right?"

"Yes, you're good to go. Thank you again, Mr. and Mrs. Richard. Enjoy the evening and our half a million lights."

I still flinched when I heard that name. Because it wasn't really mine. Marc put his arm around me, and we walked into the village. As we walked, his hand curved around my hip, his fingers resting there. Lights covered the historic Cajun buildings in the village. They had animations of Santa and there were carnival rides and a Santa with whom the kids could take pictures. On the ground was fake snow and, for the first time in the season, a nip in the air.

I rubbed my arms to warm them. "Drat, I should have checked the weather. Sofia's going to get cold."

"Not an issue." He called ahead and directed us to the gift store, *Le Magasin*. We bought *Noël au Village* sweatshirts for everyone. I helped Sofia and her best-friend, my cousin, Bailey Marie, put on their matching sweatshirts. After we were decked out in our holiday gear, we headed to listen to the music in the huge barn. The children drank hot chocolate, after which they ran to wait in line to talk to Santa. I trailed behind them. Marc came up and handed me a mug *not* filled with hot chocolate, as I assumed.

Sniffing my drink, my lips curved up at the aroma of wine and spices. My eyes met Marc's hazel ones. "*Vin chaud*?" He nodded. Hot mulled wine was my favorite winter treat. Only, I went to *Noël au Village* every year, and I have never found *vin chaud* anywhere at any time.

"A little bird told me you liked it. Also, try this." He handed me a warm pretzel. My sister apparently spilled my secrets.

I bit into the warm, salty pretzel. It's yeasty goodness spread warmth throughout my system. Add to that the sweet tang of the *vin chaud* and I was one happy camper.

"Tasty?" Marc asked. I nodded and took another bite. "Excellent, because I need you mellow for what's coming." As he said that, I noticed Kevin Babineaux, my friend Renee's brother, walk out with Hercule Trahan.

"Lawyers, guns, and money, an ominous sign. I shoulda known I wouldn't get to enjoy my snack in peace?" I murmured to myself.

"It's time for some answers." Marc said. Mr. Trahan and Kevin nodded to Marc. They headed over to the Castille House and had Marc's men set up the front porch for us. Once the children had had a chance to talk to Santa, they took their guards and went to ride the carnival rides. The adults, assured of their safety, made their way to the Castille house.

"Good evening," Mr. Trahan said. "We have some news."

"Let's get this over with. What is going on and why are my kids being targeted?" Beau asked him.

Kevin handed us each a summary sheet. "Essentially, a great-great-great-great-grandfather of Armand, Kayleigh, and the *Littles* had some specific requirements that heirs had to sign in order to receive their inheritance. Kayleigh's father and uncle signed this contract years ago to receive their equal shares of the fortune."

I frowned. "That makes no sense. My father has always relied on Nonc Bill for money."

Hercule corrected me. "That, my dear, is an under the table deal. Legally, your father is very wealthy."

With a blink, I tried to make sense of it. "If he were rich, Claire would be in a better facility and we wouldn't be relying on the kindness of Nonc Bill."

Kevin interrupted, "We think he might be being blackmailed."

I nodded at that. "Sounds like typical Nonc Bill's M.O. So Armand, the Littles, and I are all heirs to this money, but Nonc Bill wants every cent to go to Brandon. To consolidate it into his legitimate progeny. Do I have that right?"

"Precisely, my dear," Mr. Hercule told me. It gave me the *frissons*.

Marc's arm came around me, warming and calming me as he added. "When we began to suspect him, Kayleigh did say everything started when his son, Brandon, was born. Fewer heirs mean more money for his son."

Kevin flipped the papers in his binder to the post-it number three. "It's worse than that. The portions are divided up equally except for the oldest son who gets a larger portion —"

Mr. Hercule continued, "—Which is why their last attempt focused on Armand, his pregnant wife, Renee, and Tanner."

"He wants us out of the way and, if not all of us, then any male heirs, Armand, Tanner, and baby Blaise." I shivered again.

"No one will get near you, any of you," Marc said, hugging me to him. The rest of the Krewe nodded. But they didn't know Nonc Bill as I did. He did *not* give up when his mind focused on a solution. He was the gator, and we were his prey.

13

First Gumbo

Marc

Beau and Shell invited everyone to their farm for Beau's dad's famous traditional first cold snap gumbo. We didn't hesitate. Being surrounded by friends and family was exactly what we needed. We loaded up the SUV and headed out to the Babineaux's compound, where Beau, Gelly, and their parents all had homes. From the porch steps of the main house, the aroma of onion, bell pepper, smoked sausage, and the nutty aroma of the roux wafted towards us. A warm, comforting scent on a chilly day. The living room was filled with a cozy warmth, courtesy of the old-fashioned gas heaters that churned out heat at an astonishing rate. Even with the door wide opened, the heat forced us to shed our coats as quickly as we could. Sofia darted towards the other Littles, who were playing with Legos on the playroom rug. Kayleigh made a beeline for the kitchen.

"Is that a Death Star?" I asked.

"Yes, *Parrain,*" Tanner told me. "I wanted to do it on my own, but Mama says there are no toys that are just for boys." Tanner hunched his shoulders and kicked the ground.

Armand, who had been lounging on the couch holding one of his twins, snickered. "I bet she didn't like you saying something was only for boys."

Tanner sighed. "She made me bring it out for everyone to play with."

I nodded, commiserating with Tanner, "Next time, kiddo, say you want to play alone. That might work better."

Tanner tilted his head, furrowed his brow, and shouted towards the bustling kitchen. "Mama, can I play with my Millennium Falcon Legos by myself in my room?"

Renee, who was holding the other twin next to Armand, whispered, "Tell her you need some alone time."

Tanner parroted her and added, "I need some alone time. Please, Mama."

Shell came into the living room, wiping her hands on a dishtowel. "Of course, *Chéri*. You head to your room and play."

Tanner whooped and hugged me and Renee. "Thank you!" Then he ran to his room.

Sofia's interest in the Legos waned, and she bounced around us, saying, "I can't wait to see how our winter garden is going."

"You have a garden at home," I grumbled. Last year, we had added a potager for vegetables and both herbs and flowers to her ever-expanding secret garden.

"I know, but that was planted by gardeners. This one I planted with Bailey Marie, Valerie, and Tanner."

"Alex didn't help?" I asked about the second youngest of Beau and Shell's children.

"Alex was more of a hindrance than a help. He kept digging out our plants until he started eating dirt. Finally, Ms. Shell grabbed him up to wash."

When Sofia said that, I heard Kayleigh's playful chuckle behind me. She had returned from the kitchen with her coat off and I read her message tee and snorted. It was a letter to Santa with claims of being good, then kinda good, then finishing with 'Fine. I'll buy my own presents.' At Sofia's last statement, Kayleigh grinned and replied, "Alex is often more of a hindrance than a help. I don't understand how Shell chases a toddler around while caring for Baby Ellie."

As I was leaving to join the Krewe outside, Kayleigh scooped up one of the twins. Aida, I believe. She embraced her tightly, while Sofia guided the older *Littles* towards the garden. I stalled for a moment, my heart stuttering as I watched Kayleigh cuddle the baby. *She's so good with children. Not that that's important.* Shaking free of my thoughts, I moved to the front porch and nodded to one of my men to follow the Littles. Outside, Beau had a pit fire going and chairs around it. Even from that distance, the aroma of gumbo from the kitchen wafted towards me. Kevin, Jeb, and Eric, Renee's brothers, were already out there, stoking the fire.

"The chicken and sausage gumbo should be ready soon," Beau informed us as we walked up to them. He called to the Littles. "Hey y'all! We have croquet set up in the front lawn" He pointed to the game and the *Littles* all ran up and grabbed a mallet. Sofia, ever my goth, chose the black mallet. I grinned at her selection. We let the children set up their own game, knowing they were safe and guarded by my men. Nevertheless, my eyes tracked the kids and scanned the surroundings for any signs of danger.

Kayleigh headed out onto the porch and joined us. She followed my eyes and patted my shoulder. "I'm sure she's safe here." That reassuring pat calmed me.

My eyebrow raised. "I seem to remember getting injured here after an attack. In point of fact, you were my EMT."

"Ah, yes. It's all coming back to me. You being a pain in the *tchu* and not listening to any of my sage advice." She sat next to me.

"C'mon." I nudged her with my foot. "No time to argue now. Let's get a libation and make some plans."

Once we scooched closer to the fire, she said, "I don't really get what kind of plans we can make."

Kevin offered his ideas. "Well, we at least figured out why your uncle is targeting the Littles. We also understand why he targeted Armand, Tanner, and the twins specifically."

"That's a lot of people to get rid of," I stated.

"Why didn't he attack me or Claire?" Kayleigh warmed her hands in the fire but shivered, anyway.

I put my arm around her to warm her. She stiffened at first, but then acquiesced and leaned into me. "He wanted to get you under his thumb. How many of his lackeys has he tried to get you to go out with? As long as he felt in control, he did not see any reason for violence. The violence only occurred when you took over Claire's care and he could no longer force you to date his lackeys. I'm sure he assumed you would settle for one of them, so he would still be in control of the funds."

She stared into the fire. "And now he has no control."

Beau said, "Plus, he's under investigation for the attacks. Stan might not testify against him, but he said enough to launch an investigation. If he was arrogant enough to think he would never get caught and used his cell phone, we can tie him to all the attacks that have happened."

Ever the voice of reason, Kevin added, "However, we need to keep in mind that this is all for Brandon. Even if he drops a bomb on us and goes to jail, the funds will still go to Brandon. He can't benefit from his crimes, but his son can. We need to be prepared for anything."

"How much money are we talking about, anyway?" Kayleigh asked Kevin.

"From our research, in terms of property, goods, and cash, it totals over a billion dollars altogether."

Kayleigh coughed. "I'm sorry. Did you say a billion? So an eighth of a billion dollars per person. Shell, math this for me."

"Half is 500 million. Quarter is 250 million. And half of that is 125 million." Shell calculated.

Armand shook his head. "Seriously, 125 million won't be enough for the kid? That's absurd."

"Greed is a disease," Marc said. "I've seen it infect many men. They stop thinking of money as a tool to do things and start thinking of it as part of their self-worth and power. They always want more power."

"As they become worse and worse humans," Gelly added.

Kevin corrected us. "You are doing the math wrong. Since Kayleigh's dad is supposed to have 500 million. She and Claire will inherit that and everyone else shares the other 500 million. Also, since she's married and can no longer marry a lackey, expect Bill to target her."

Kayleigh shook her head in disbelief. "It's a crazy will."

"Actually, it's worse than the Napoleonic laws of succession. Those gave half of the money to the wife and then divided the remaining funds amongst any child, legitimate or illegitimate. In this will, Brandon's mother and yours, Kayleigh, get nothing," Kevin added.

"I'm starting to really dislike my ancestor," Kayleigh groused.

Shell nodded. "Right back at you. How could he not foresee that this would turn greedy kids against their relatives?"

"He probably knew. It was written after 1869, which is when Darwin put the phrase 'survival of the fittest' into the fifth edition of *Origin of the Species,*" Etienne, ever the scholar, intoned.

"Nonc Bill thinks he's the fittest? I don't think so. But I'm worried about what my dad did that was worth giving up 500 million dollars." Kayleigh massaged her temples.

"I already have PIs working on that." I told her.

"I'm not sure I want to know," Kayleigh said.

I side-hugged her. "Forewarned is forearmed."

14

Cooling Down = Heating Up

Kayleigh

Upon our return from the Babineaux farm, Sofia organized us to get 'the basic' Christmas decorating done. We searched the garage for boxes marked 'Christmas decorations.'

"These boxes?" I asked.

Sofia shook her head and pointed to some old, worn boxes. "Those are the ones we use."

We spent an hour putting up a gold tree, and stockings on the hearth, and mistletoe. We worked on it alone, just us three. Marc made it clear that he wanted no help whatsoever from his staff. This was a family activity.

I examined the tree. It didn't fill the space. "Do you plan to get a real pine tree, too?"

Sofia nodded. "Of course, this one we keep up and redecorate after Christmas. So it is our Christmas-slash-Epiphany-slash-Mardi Gras-tree. After Christmas day, we'll replace the red with purple for Epiphany and the start of Mardi Gras." Her jump when she said Mardi Gras gave me the warm fuzzies.

"What's left to do, Sof?" Marc asked after he lifted her to place an angel on the top of the decorated tree.

She ran to the last box we'd carried in and flung it open. "Mistletoe!"

I glanced inside the box. "That's a *lot* of mistletoe. Are you planning a kissing party?"

Sofia laughed. "We put it all over the house. Today we just need to decorate the living room and hang the front door mistletoe. I'll work with the *au pair* later to put the rest up."

"Lucky *au pair*," I whispered.

Marc clapped me on the back. "C'mon, let's get this over with."

"Daddy, the journey is more important than the destination, remember?"

Marc grinned over at her. "Right you are, my mini-Buddha."

He saw me tilt my head and explained. "We've been reading the *Tao of Pooh* at night."

I chucked. "Funny! Our bedtime story is *Le petit prince*. She is a little goth philosopher."

Sofia smiled, "*Ce qui est important est toujours invisible.* The decorations are pretty, but that's not the important part. Plus, I'm more than a philosopher. I dance too!"

Marc hugged her. Then he grabbed the ladder one of his men had fetched for him, and climbed up it. For safety, and safety alone, I held the ladder in place. I did not, at all, cast furtive glances at the most perfect *tchu* I'd ever seen. *Strong, built, and sexy, with just a hint of nerd. Those glasses. Gah!*

Shivering, I handed him the mistletoe. I blinked to remember our pre-leer conversation. *Oh yes, Sofia's brainpower.* "A regular Renaissance kid," I added, and Sofia giggled.

Then she smirked as Marc descended the ladder. "Daddy, you're now under the mistletoe with Ms. Kayleigh. You know the rules."

As I peered up at Marc, he leaned down to give me what I thought would be a peck on the cheek. I closed my eyes in anticipation. Instead of a buss on the cheek, our lips touched and, just like that, conflagration. The world disappeared, and there was only Marc. His hands framed my head as he held me in place. His tongue drove in and mine mimicked his movement. My body heated and my clothes became a nuisance. I wanted them gone. A throat cleared and penetrated our lust-filled haze. My eyes blinked a few times, as Marc moved his head away. I loosened the grip I didn't realize I had on his shirt.

I looked over at Sofia, who stared at us. "Umm."

"Time for bed!" Marc said, and my heat rose again. "Sofia. Time for bed, Sofia."

Don't get ideas. "Right, I need to get to bed as well. I'll see you both in the morning."

"Don't forget to come and read to me," Sofia reminded us both.

After reading to Sofia, I snuck away to my room, threw on my PJs and robe, and got ready for bed. A soft knock sounded. When cracked the door opened, I saw Marc holding two steaming mugs. I opened the door wider for him to enter. As he passed by me, the aroma of mint filled the space. He knew my routine. I always made myself mint tea before bed.

He handed me a mug. "Can we talk?"

"Yes, but I really do need to go to bed." His eyes flared. "To sleep. I need to get to sleep."

He blinked and took a breath. "Fair enough. Let's discuss our agreement first."

"Oh yay! Contracts. Give me that tea." I sank into a chair in my reading nook, took the tea with both hands. With a nod of my chin, I indicated the other chair for Marc.

Marc set his tea on the side table and sat in my reading chair. "About our agreement—"

"—I suppose you'll make out like a bandit on it now that I'm in line for a fortune. I remember a clause about the percentage of income. Lucky you had me sign it before I knew I would be rich."

He handed me a document from his back pocket.

"What's this?"

"A revised relationship agreement to ensure that you and your children will always get your money."

"I was teasing. You would never date someone for their money." I smiled at him.

"Why not?"

"Well, first, because you wouldn't ever want to date a gold digger. I've heard stories."

Annoyance flashed in his eyes. "What stories?"

With a shrug of my shoulders, I said, "Just stories about you and your aversion to gold diggers."

"It comes hard earned. I'm aware you're not a gold digger. Kayleigh."

"I'll be worth more than you soon." I snickered.

Marc laughed at that. "Possibly." He rose. "I'll let you get to sleep." Before he walked out the door, I felt his warm breath on my cheek as he leaned in for a quick peck. I took advantage and turned my face. I wanted that fire again. The kiss deepened and his hands moved to my waist, gripping me. When his tongue licked my lower lip and then filled my mouth, I lost all coherent thought. We lingered there, and I reveled in this novel sensation of heat and storms.

Suddenly, Marc pulled away. "Kayleigh, we need to stop." I moved in closer, and he stepped back. "Don't. My self-control is threadbare."

I stepped forward again, erasing that distance. "Excellent. That's what I'm hoping for." I nipped his ear.

"Careful what you wish for." He picked me up and carried me to my bed. For an instant, he left me as he hurried to lock my bedroom door. When he neared, I wrapped my legs around him and pulled him close, savoring the weight of him crushing me. I trapped him with my calves. With an effort, he pulled back from me for an instant as he ripped off my PJ top.

"Hey!"

"I'll replace it." And off came my bra as well. He inhaled once as he looked his fill, and then he cupped my breasts as he nibbled and sucked on my nipples, giving me an indescribable sensation.

As he lifted for a breath, I said, "Clothes off." At that moment, it was the most I could muster.

He grinned, his dimples on display. "Your wish." He tugged off his shirt.

"Lose the pants as well." He pulled them off and reached into his pocket for his wallet and the condom that he kept in there. As he set the condom on the nightstand, I started to wiggle out of my PJ bottoms. But he placed his hand over my stomach, his big bronzed hand with his Michaelangelo forearms. Staring at that hand against my ivory skin made my insides clench. I turned to see him naked and fully aroused. *That won't fit* flitted through my brain.

"You sure about this?" Marc asked. He must have seen my expression.

"Yes. Absolutely." I nodded, but my muscles tensed and I averted my gaze.

He pulled back. "Um hum. In that case, tell me what you want, what you like."

I sighed. *Marc was always difficult*. I turned to him and pouted. "I want a little less talk."

He grinned all the way to his dimples again. "And a lot more action?"

"Yes, please."

He covered me, balancing on those forearms, those wonderful forearms. First, he leaned toward me and kissed my lips, my earlobes, my neck, and my breasts. He paused there. "You sure you don't want to give me some direction?"

"You're doing great." I encouraged him.

He kissed across my belly, licking into my belly button, then descending until he reached my core. There, he found my clit with his finger as he licked into me. I lost myself then in his touch and his scent. I grabbed on to the brass headboard, trying to find purchase ... find reality. But to no avail. When one of his fingers entered me, my grasp on reality evaporated. I arched, falling and seeing stars as I cried out.

"It's clear we will need to move to a soundproofed room."

I gasped, trying to catch my breath. "You ... have ... one of those?"

"I have a few, but we will talk about that later." He grabbed the condom off the nightstand and ripped it open with his teeth. My eyes widened. I couldn't help but notice he had grown even larger. *There's no way that will fit.* I tensed.

"What's wrong? I just got you all loose and now you're tensing up on me."

"I'm ummm." Unsure of how to break the news to him that it wouldn't fit.

Marc's dimple emerged. "We're made for each other, Kayleigh. Let me relax you again." He used his fingers, his magic fingers, on me again. At the same time, he kissed from my lips, down the side of my neck and to my breasts as he caressed my core, flicking and pinching my clit. As I crested, he positioned himself against me and inched into me. *This isn't too bad.* Then he surged forward, and I cried out in pain.

"Dammit. I knew it. You didn't fit." Hitting his back with my fist, I squirmed around, trying to find a more comfortable position.

"Ah Kayleigh, you need to stop moving." His hand moved between us and began fingering me as I searched for a better position. I was on the brink of something, I could sense it, when Marc lost control. He pistoned his hips while his fingers dug into me. I was so close. On the precipice of something, Marc shouted, strained against me, and then flopped on top of me, like a dead fish.

"Drat!"

He chuckled at that. "Perhaps if you had told me that this was your first time."

"It seemed like need to know information and you didn't need to know." I turned my head to the side.

Marc pinched my chin and turned my face back to him. "I could've improved the experience for you."

"It wasn't terrible." I shrugged. *I mean, it's not 'romance novel' good, but it hadn't been terrible.*

"Yes, 'drat' is actually high praise from you." He kissed me on the forehead.

"We didn't fit. That was the problem."

"No, we fit. Had I known it was your first time, I'd have optimized the experience." He rolled off of me.

I crossed my arms over my chest. "Shouldn't you always do the most possible to optimize the experience?"

"Not having this argument now." He popped out of bed and made his way to the bathroom. He came back with a washcloth.

"What's that for?"

"For you." He moved toward me.

I stopped him and grabbed the washcloth. "I can take care of it myself," I told him, no doubt beet red.

"It's my responsibility." He quickly snatched the washcloth and gently placed the warm cloth on me, and I couldn't help but feel the soothing warmth easing my soreness. But warm water couldn't assuage my shame.

"This is embarrassing." I turned my face into the pillow.

"Yes, it's embarrassing that you didn't tell me you'd never had sex before." He brushed my hair from my face as his other hand pressed on the cloth.

I glanced at him and shrugged. "Never with a man."

Both his eyebrows lifted. "Oh, you swing that way. Do you?"

I sat up. "What, no. I mean ... I have Bob."

"Bob?"

His frowny face made me laugh. "My battery-operated boyfriend, BOB. He does an excellent job."

Marc threw the washcloth onto the bathroom floor, got in bed, and pulled me towards him. He felt warm and smelled of cedar trees and soap. "Next time, I'll see if I can top BOB."

"You want there to be a next time?"

"There will no doubt be a next time. Now, go to sleep." I snuggled close into him. He spooned around me and I tried to get as close as possible, until he said, "Stop wiggling or that next time will come sooner rather than later."

I grinned, took a deep sniff of him, and fell asleep. Later, I woke to Marc cuddled up next to me. I studied his sleeping form. He had protected me, protected my sister, and put up with my endless snark. That deserved a reward.

15

Old Wounds

Marc

I woke with warmth radiating through me. Stretching with a smile, as the sun shimmered through the window sheers. I felt rested and something else: lightness, peace? I wasn't sure, but I liked it. I thought back on the previous evening. It had been ages since I'd let my guard down enough to sleep with someone in my own home. Of course, that's where Kayleigh was living. Still, it was a big step. Any other woman post-Tracy, I'd rented hotel rooms, and left immediately afterwards. I rolled over to take Kayleigh in my arms, but the bed was empty. Which was a shame, but baby steps. Grabbing my clothes, I made my way to the shower. "Siri, play Swamp pop." "Shake" by Ryan Foret and the Foret Tradition played. *Perfect.* I shook to the beat while I showered. *Things are falling into place.*

At first I didn't notice anything awry. After my shower, I dressed in my room, and then headed to the kitchen. That's where I usually found my girls. Sofia and Kayleigh always met up there in the morning, their laughter echoing through the air. The kitchen was cheery, filled with the aroma of cookies and fresh coffee, but no one was there.

As I poured my morning joe, I called out. "Anyone home?"

Sofia skipped towards me. "We're in the living room, Daddy. We have a surprise for you. Close your eyes." I took a single gulp of coffee to jolt my system and then set my mug on the counter. While I needed the caffeine, I didn't want to delay Sofia's surprise. I closed my eyes and held out my hand to her. She grasped it, and with an eager titter, led me to the living room. I smelled the pine tree, the wood fire, and the lavender/cinnamon scent of Kayleigh. I grinned, anxious to see their surprise. I heard my parents' voices as well. So, it was a family surprise. It was a good sign that Kayleigh got along with my parents. I had something up my sleeve for her as well. We could get our surprises together.

Sofia squeezed my hand. "Okay, Daddy. Open your eyes."

I opened my eyes and froze. My breath stopped and the warmth that had surrounded me all morning dissipated in a cloud of red rage.

My mom greeted me and hugged me. "Good morning, sleepyhead. What do you think?"

My arms closed automatically around her, while my eyes scanned the room. I tried to speak, but my throat tightened. Devoid of speech, my words swallowed by an overwhelming fire of betrayal. There in every corner of my house was every effing ornament that Tracy made me get, when I was in my fake happy mode. Before I learned of her perfidy. Now, my idiocy was strewn across my living room.

Sofia bounced on the balls of her feet. "Kayleigh found all these ornaments in the garage. Aren't they great, Daddy?"

I still couldn't speak, but my dad covered for me. "Yes, the ladies even made sugar cookie ornaments to add to the tree."

It was my worst Christmas nightmare come to life. There was the nativity scene that Tracy had cooed over while she pretended to be carrying my child. Atop the tree was the star that Tracy and I bought, the star she guaranteed we'd use when our grandchildren came along. As she was screwing my lowdown cousin. The rage swept through me. Everywhere I turned was her betrayal. Even, I'm ashamed to admit, when I looked at my excited, beautiful daughter.

Kayleigh must've sensed it, "Mr. Lionel, Ms. Sue, thank you so much for your help. Let's make plans to have a holiday get together before you come over for Christmas day. Does that sound good?"

My parents nodded at Kayleigh. Mom kissed Sofia, promising to come back and help her with her Christmas gift wrapping. My dad lifted her up and spun her around, making her giggle.

"See you soon, snuggle bug," he told her, heading out to the foyer. As they walked by, my dad, sensing the tension, looked me in the eye and said, "Don't be a *couillon*, Marc. You have something good here."

Part of my brain processed that I'm sure, just not the one currently in control of my body. I think I nodded at him, but I couldn't remember.

In the silence that followed my parents' departure, Sofia noticed the tension. "Daddy, is something wrong?"

I cleared my throat. "Everything will be okay, Sofia. Why don't you go and plan our next holiday event? The house is beautiful. You did a great job."

Tears welled in Sofia's eyes. "But Daddy, you're mad at me. I can tell."

"He's not." Kayleigh said, hugging Sofia and shooing her out of the room.

At the same time, I repeated, "I'm not, sweetie."

Sofia, taking me at my word, gave me a perfunctory hug before she left and went to her room. "Okay, Daddy. I'm going to plan our boat decorations for the Christmas on the Teche parade," she said as she skipped out.

That should've worked. Her excitement and joy should have knocked me out of my funk. But surrounded by the wreckage that Tracy had left behind, I could *not* break free.

Kayleigh glared at me. "I'm not sure what's wrong with you, but you better snap out of it. If you're angry that we slept together, I assure you that after this 'morning after glow'," she quoted with her fingers, "we will *not* be repeating that mistake. I didn't make you sleep with me and if you don't want me decorating, then that should have been stated in your stupid relationship agreement. You're a real *tchu*, you know that?"

Again, her words processed somewhere in my brain as absolutely true, but they did not break through my rage. I snapped at her, "It's *not t*hat. Where did you get *these* decorations? I thought I had thrown them out."

Kayleigh grimaced. "Why would you throw them out? They're beautiful. What else did you decorate with?"

"You had no right to just pull my things out of storage and start using them."

With her chin set, Kayleigh gave a monotone reply. "You're absolutely right. I'm not really a part of this family. I'm just here through the holidays, but you stipulated that I was to do holiday things with Sofia. Christmas decorating is a holiday tradition and decorating was on the approved list that is clearly posted on the fridge. If you had a problem with it, you should have mentioned that earlier."

"I don't give a damn if you decorate, but *not* with these decorations!" I yelled.

"I'm sorry. The rest of the world keeps Christmas decorations in boxes marked 'Christmas decorations' in their garages and attics. When I saw a box in your garage marked 'Christmas Decorations', I had the audacity to assume that was what we needed to decorate for Christmas." That last part she enunciated like I was a toddler. That did not improve my mood.

"Well, you should have asked." I grabbed up the worst offenders in terms of my pain, searching for boxes to dump them into. Kayleigh swiftly pulled out the storage boxes from behind the couch. I wasted no time in gathering the decorations and flinging them inside the box.

"Never fear. I won't repeat that mistake. In fact, I won't make any more mistakes in *your* home, about *your* family, again." Distant with only a slight quiver in her voice, Kayleigh left me to my task and headed to her room.

Throwing the nativity scene in the box, the resulting crash was a balm for my soul. I threw in the other offending decorations. As I finished, I noticed Kayleigh with a backpack heading toward the front door. I followed her. "What's happening, Kayleigh? Where're you going?"

"Funny, I was wondering what happened as well. You don't seem inclined to explain. Since you can't seem to make up your mind as to where I fit in this equation, in your family. I'm going to stay with *my* family. Your relationship agreement wasn't clear, and I'm tired of always being the outsider." As she turned, clothes fell out of her broken backpack. Tears streamed from her eyes as she gathered the clothes and shoved them back in. "I'll get the rest of my things later." She wiped her eyes with the back of her hands and headed to the door.

As she walked away, I couldn't breathe or think. "If you leave, it will be a clear violation of the relationship agreement."

"So, sue me!" She stormed out, slamming the door.

I sat on the couch, rocking, when Sofia entered.

"What did you do Daddy? Why are you mad?" She climbed up beside me and leaned her cheek against my shoulder.

"It's not you, *Chérie*." My arm enveloped her and squeezed.

"Is it Ms. Kayleigh? Because all the decorations were my idea and the cookies were Mawmaw's idea. Ms. Kayleigh only helped."

I nodded my head in my hands. I knew that.

"Will Ms. Kayleigh be okay?" My head raised like a meerkat. Paul was on duty today and I had just sent Kayleigh into the world unprotected, with a target on her back.

"I'm an idiot." My darling daughter nodded and patted my shoulder while I got on the phone and tried to fix things.

16

Rage Decorating

Kayleigh

"**I** diot! The *couillon fils d' putain*, except his mother is a gem, so I will stick with *couillon*," I mumbled to no one in particular as the Uber drove me to the library. The driver glanced at the rear-view mirror. Probably to ensure that I wasn't dangerous. He looked vaguely familiar. I shook that off and concentrated on my list of ways I could maim Marc *Couillon* Richard.

Getting down at the library, I used my keys to enter the building. I'd called in a personal day when Sofia had asked me to help her decorate the house today. I even called Shell to inform her that Sofia would be absent from school.

"One day of hooky is good for kids. Have a fun Sofia Day," she had said.

Today was *not* beneficial for Sofia. Unless children witnessing their trusted adults having a knock-down-drag-out fight was good for kids. *Pauvre* Sofia. She thought her daddy'd be so happy. I thought so too. I still don't understand what happened. What's the big deal? Who cares which boxes of decorations you use? "If you don't want decorations used, then get rid of them

or at the very least don't mark them as 'Christmas Decorations."
I told Marc. He wasn't there, but it needed to be said ... again.

Whatever, for now I was decorating the library. I knew I
was safe from any scolding because that was my typical task at
the start of December and because librarians aren't *couillon* like
Marc. I turned on my Christmas playlist and inhaled the scent
of old books, hoping that'd snap me out of my mood. Once
the music began, I made myself an extra strong cup of steaming
coffee in our coffee machine. It had been a rough morning.
I used one of the fancy cappuccino pods. After a big slug of
coffee, I pulled out the Christmas wreaths, ornaments, and
lights from the boxes marked 'Christmas Decorations'. Instead
of making me joyous, the explosion of gold, red, and green
decorations made me fume. *See Marc, Couillon, everyone labels
the decorations they plan to decorate with that way!* My internal
argument with him must have conjured the beast because the
moment I started decorating, he walked into the library. *Drat!
I wish I worked at a private library where I could lock out the
riffraff, aka Marc.*

I turned my back to him and snarked, "Oh, I'm sorry. Am I
not to decorate with any Christmas ornaments here either? My
mistake, see how the boxes are labeled *'Christmas Decorations'*.
Silly me."

"No. I mean—"

"—Tough. This is my house. I do what I want." Whirling
away, I left him there, and started decorating another section of
the library.

Marc picked up my coffee cup and followed me. "This is a
library, not a house."

I hung a wreath on an office door and turned to give him
my best speaking-to-a-toddler voice. "Very good. This is a
library and not a house. That is a bookshelf." I pointed to the
bookshelf. "And I'm the librarian, so in this building I make the
rules. Now, be quiet or you'll have to leave."

He moved closer. "I wanted to apologize." He handed me my coffee.

I accepted the cup and took a sip, swallowing the warm coffee, along with my tears. "I'm sure you do. Your behavior was abhorrent. We decorated your house to make you happy, and you berated me. Worse, you made Sofia feel bad. Did you apologize to her?"

Marc nodded. "She told me to go and apologize to you."

"At least someone in your house has manners. Not a problem. After this morning, I'll no longer have anything to do with you. Please deliver my car today, outside the library, and I'll be out of your hair." I continued decorating. Having done it for years, I was on autopilot. I knew where everything went, and I could focus on those movements instead of my rage at Marc's behavior.

"What about Sofia? She'll miss you."

"Don't try to emotionally blackmail me. I am a pro at dealing with that; I've been dealing with that my entire life. Sofia will see me when you bring her to get books and for story time. Like before."

He tried a different tack. "I can't protect you as well if you're not under my roof, especially if you are living in a car who knows where in the city."

"You sure this isn't about having a convenient woman around?" That truth hit deep. I was an idiot. I got sucked into our make-believe family. My love for Sofia and wish to have a real family, one that truly cared about me, had led me to give myself to a man that didn't care at all. I pulled out my phone and ordered another Uber.

"It's not like that." Marc put his hands in his pockets and hunched over.

Bullshit. You can't play the wounded party here. "Oh really? I sleep with you and then you decide you can shit all over me for doing what you *asked* me to do. For doing what was written in your stupid relationship agreement. Plus, plus, you knew that decorating for Christmas was on the list and you showed me where the Christmas decorations were located." Surprised that steam was not coming from my ears, I moved away to decorate elsewhere. Over my shoulder, I tossed. "I'm not anyone's punching bag. Not physically and not metaphorically. So you and the rest of your kind can get out."

He followed me and got in my face. "I'm not the same as Stan or your uncle. I would never hurt you or use your love for family to blackmail you. I'd never do that. You're the one that overreacted and left."

"You think that, don't you? That you can just gaslight me. Pretend you did nothing wrong. What? So, I'm the bad guy for raising my voice a little when I'm mistreated? Don't overreact, little lady." I did my best interpretation of Nonc Bill and every other man that had screwed me over and then taunted me for reacting to their awful behavior. "*Piqué-toi*. For your information, you have hurt me a lot. And you just tried to use my love of Sofia to get your way." I was done, and I meant done, with being a doormat. At his hesitation, I knew I had hit on his exact approach. *Dumbass.* Checking my phone to see where my Uber was, I needed to get away.

Marc backtracked. "I'm sorry. You're right. I'm a complete *tchu*. Can we talk?"

"We've been talking, but I can't be around you right now." I dropped the un-used decorations into the box. "Look, it's marked 'Christmas decorations.' I wonder what I should do with the items in this box? *Couillon*." I put up the box and walked outside. The Uber I ordered was already there. As I opened the car door, I realized the Uber was driven by one of Marc's men. That's where I recognized my first driver.

"You moonlighting as an Uber driver?" I asked as I got in.

"I am today, apparently." He smiled at me. "Where to?"

"Happy Place assisted living home." I needed to see my sister and decorate her room without having to deal with a grumpy bear.

On the way to the Happy Place, a text came through.

Marc: I have a present for you. I was planning to give it to you this morning.

Is it your head on a pike?

Marc: Kayleigh, please listen.

You're texting, I can't listen. *Couillon*.

Marc: I have a surprise for you. One I planned before the "incident".

You mean the incident where you were an unreasonable *tchu* and treated me like crap?

Marc: Yes.

Well, maybe in a month or two when the mad wears off, you can give it to me.

Marc: It might be sooner than that.

Piqué-toi

And with that, I silenced my phone, laid my head against the headrest, and closed my eyes. See, this mess was why I avoided dating seriously my whole life. *Not worth it.*

17

Prison Break

Marc

As I entered the Happy Place assisted living home, I nodded to the guard/Uber driver I had assigned to watch Kayleigh. I handed the head nurse the paperwork that Kevin had created for me. Her eyebrows raised, but she got to work at once.

"You know what you're getting into, right? Claire is a dear, but she takes a lot of work," the nurse said as she walked me to Claire's room.

I dipped my chin. "Yes. I have a team of medical experts on call and ready to work with her."

"Do you need me to phone for hospital transport?" she asked.

I shook my head and glanced out the window at the enormous van parked there.

"She has a visitor now." The nurse looked at the paperwork. "Your wife. Ms. Kayleigh has been her only visitor since the accident. I mean, besides you. *Pauvre bête,* you would think her parents would at least come to see her once. They can't be bothered, it seems. Retiring early in Florida and not even keeping up your insurance on your child. At least Ms. Kayleigh was able to remedy that." She shook her head.

Kayleigh wasn't only Claire's sister. She was the only person who took care of her until now. I nodded to my team that came in and we headed to Claire's room. I listened through the door.

"Can you believe! All I did was make cookies with his daughter and parents and decorate his whole damn house. For that I get yelled at." I imagined her pacing the room as she complained about me.

"Maybe he wasn't mad at you. He seems like a nice guy." *Thank you, sister-in-law.*

"What would you know?"

"Marc stops in to see me all the time. He has since you told him about me."

"He has? What do you two talk about? You're into art and he's into guns."

"What do you two talk about?" Claire countered.

"Sofia mostly. Actually, he rarely tells me anything about himself. You know things like why using Christmas decorations from a box marked 'Christmas decorations' would put him in a fury."

"Well, you should definitely talk about that. Marc and I discuss my art a lot. He has been brainstorming ways that I can do my creating without the use of my appendages. Which, as you know, are useless, or at least as he says, are not useful, yet."

"Exactly. He's right about that. Once we get you some better PT, you'll improve. For now, they're not working," Kayleigh said.

"Possibly for now, possibly forever. I have to face reality and figure out how to move on with my life. That's what Marc says. Don't give me that look. It's not a bad thing living my life in the present rather than waiting for the life I used to have."

I opened the door on that. "Where have I heard that before?" Claire smiled while Kayleigh's eyes narrowed.

Claire said, "From you."

Kayleigh pointed towards the door behind me. "Get out!"

"Can't," I told her. "Today's the big day."

"What day?" Kayleigh asked, but I just grinned at Claire.

She glowed. "It's Prison Break Day? Already! I thought it would take forever."

My men came in and started packing up Claire's personal items. Claire's eyes glowed.

Kayleigh followed me as I went through the bathroom drawers. "Wait, what do you mean, prison break?"

"He's getting me out of here, Kayleigh. I'm moving in with you at Marc's."

"He conveniently forgot to tell me about that when I *moved out* this morning."

"You moved out? Why?" Claire asked.

"You heard how he treated me." Kayleigh dropped into the chair next to Claire, crossed her arms, and *boudeyed*. [pouted]

"Yes, that was unacceptable. Explain Marc." Claire ordered, in nearly the same tone as her sister. I fought valiantly not to smile.

Kayleigh's little rose bud mouth swelled in a pout. "You call him Marc? You barely know him."

"He's my brother-in-law."

"Temporarily," Kayleigh grumbled.

"Well then, this prison break might be temporary, but I don't care. I want to live now and this place is not conducive to living." Claire's face glowed as she watched us pack up her world.

"They don't treat you well here? I mean, aside from the two weeks when Nonc Bill was in charge." Tinker Bell did not like hearing that her sister wasn't happy.

"They treat me fine, worrywart. The nurses and orderlies are overworked and underpaid. I want to be around regular people, around you and your life."

I tried not to smirk as Kayleigh narrowed her eyes at me again. "Fine, I'll go back."

My lungs relaxed. I hadn't realized they were so tense.

"On one condition." Because, with Kayleigh, nothing was ever simple.

"Of course there's a condition." I loaded up the last of Claire's things and handed them off to one of my men. "Alright, hit me with it."

Kayleigh moved over to me. I'd say she got in my face, but she was a foot too short for that. Still, the move was effective. "You have to tell me what happened this morning."

I averted my eyes, a sure tell. "I lost my temper, that's all."

Kayleigh raised her hand. "I call bullshit."

"I second that call," Claire added. Demonstrating how my life was about to be outnumbered by women in a big way.

Huffing out a breath, I said, "Fine. You ride back with me and I'll explain what happened."

"But, point of order, just to clarify to everyone in the room, I did nothing to deserve your wrath. Correct?" She poked me in the chest to emphasize that statement.

"You did nothing to deserve my wrath." And I'd never win an argument again. I'm not sure why that thought cheered me up.

"In fact," Kayleigh continued, because winning an argument wasn't enough. "I was being kind and considerate and doing exactly what I told you I would do when you rained fire down on my head."

I bit my cheek. "Yes, you were in the right, 100%, and I was all in the wrong."

Kayleigh nodded. "As long as that's clarified."

I looked over, and Claire was smirking at me.

"What?"

"Nothing. Just looking at the next fifty years of your life."

I closed my eyes. That's what I was thinking. She was probably right. Hopefully right. We'd see. As we were traveling, I explained everything to Kayleigh. She already knew about Sofia's parentage, but I don't think she understood the depth of Tracy's perfidy.

"Your cousin?"

"Yes."

"You still in touch with this perfidious cousin?"

"Actually, I believe Tracy told him that we broke up. She just pulled off her engagement ring without so much as a by your leave and slept with him. He died in Afghanistan. So I can't really be mad at him. Tracy has moved on."

"Yay, I'm the lucky one that gets your wrath. I won't even talk about how this morning's response made me question what we did the last night. You made me regret my action. Actions I wasn't sure I should have taken in the first place."

"I know, I'm a complete *tchu*."

"Yes, total ass. No way around it." She thought for a moment. "I'll move back in, but no more blow-ups blaming me for something someone else did to you. You can be mad at me for the crap I pull, but no transferring your rage to me. Also, if it is on the list and I do it, you get zero say into how it's done."

"Agreed. I'll change the relationship agreement." I pulled out my phone, but Kayleigh stayed my hand.

"Nope. This is a verbal agreement and you'll have to T R U S T me." She spelled it out.

"I think—"

She shook her head. "—No, you don't get a say. What you think is inconsequential. You want me back. You agree, verbally, to my terms and we shake on it."

"Fine, I agree." I gave her my free hand, and she shook it. Then she leaned over, kissed my cheek and said, "Dumbass."

When we got back to the house, I had Claire and her helpers drive to the back room I had set up near Kayleigh's and Sofia's rooms. Kayleigh and I came in the front door.

"Kayleigh!!" Sofia ignored me and ran to hug her. "I thought you were leaving us. Please don't leave. I'm sorry."

"You didn't do anything wrong; neither did I." Then she gave me a pointed look.

"I'm sorry, Sofia. I acted irrationally. Neither you, my parents, nor Kayleigh did anything wrong. I've been a grump."

"You have." Sofia reached over and hugged me. That is when I noticed all the ornaments were gone.

"You took them down," I said.

"They made you sad," she answered simply.

Kayleigh squeezed Sofia's shoulder with her hand. "We will buy and make some new ones. Come meet my sister." She turned as they were heading out and whispered to me, "Call your parents." Then she and Sofia skipped off, hand in hand.

I watched them, Tink and my goth Pippi Longstocking, and thought that I needed to keep Kayleigh in our lives. I pulled out my phone and hit the button to call my parents.

My mom didn't even let me speak. "You *T-tchu*, I hope you resolved everything."

"Yes, mom. Kayleigh's back and her sister is here too. You should come and visit."

"I won't get my head bitten off for doing nice things for you?" My lip quirked. She and Kayleigh had matching attitudes. "No ma'am. I'll be on my best behavior."

My dad got on then. "Don't shame me, son. I raised you better than what I saw this morning."

"Yes, sir. Kayleigh put me in my place."

"As she should. You made a good choice, even if the way you married her was non-traditional. You need to keep that one."

"It's temporary."

"Make it permanent," he ordered.

"I'm not sure I know how to do that."

18

Boat Decorating

Kayleigh

Once we got Claire back home, Marc deposited her in a room that he had created just for her. It had a ramp with a paved pathway to the secret garden and a motorized wheelchair so she could get there independently. He installed a motorized bed that allowed her to get in and out of bed more easily and a wheelchair-accessible shower. He put a necklace around Claire's neck.

"Kayleigh and I want you to be independent, but if you need help. I have nursing staff on call, including my cousin, to help you out. Just press this button here," he told her. I explored the room as he explained to Claire about its features, the PT schedule, and the in-home doctor visits he had set up for her. This whole time, this I'm-in-charge-and-doing-it-for-your-own-protection lout had been creating a perfect room for my sister. I turned to watch Claire beam up at Marc, enchanted by her hero. I glanced down before he could notice tears in my own eyes. My heart thudded in my chest.

After Claire's rescue, détente was achieved. We were able to live together, establishing new routines that kept the peace.

Sofia and I breakfasted in Claire's room each morning. Over bites of egg white veggie omelettes and fresh sourdough toast (Agnès was determined to get Claire healthy again), we would discuss our projects. Claire's goals were to get better and put together an art portfolio for her college admission packets. She talked of her treatments, physical therapies, and strategies that she was learning to create her art. Currently, she was painting, sculpting, and drawing with her mouth and her hands. Although, her hands still lacked the fine motor control to create art up to Claire's standards.

"I'm hoping that I can create enough to do my senior show." Claire had been finishing up her final year at the Louisiana School for Math Sciences and the Arts when we got in the wreck. I remembered how happy and relieved I'd been when she had been accepted to the boarding gifted program. The school took the responsibility of her room and board from my shoulders. Plus, I knew she was safe there. She showed us the work she'd done using different mediums: painting, pencil sketch, and etchings on clay tablets. "Like Hammurabi and the ancient Babylonians," Claire said.

Sofia bit into the contraband *pain au chocolat* she snuck from the kitchen and asked with her mouth full, "Whose Hammurabi?"

With her hand held out for a *pain au chocolat* pastry of her own, Claire answered. "Hammurabi was an ancient Babylonian king who wrote down all the kingdom's laws, or, as we call them, the Code of Hammurabi. It was one of the first example of human written work. The oldest deciphered writing of significant length. It included all the laws of Babylon like property rights, family law, even justice in their legal system." Sofia handed her a pastry, and they gleefully finished their sweet treat s.

I beamed at my little sister. Her head was always full of fun, useless facts. And, based on how her eyes glowed with hope, maybe not so useless. I bit my cheek and counted backwards to avoid any tears. "It's amazing, Claire."

"Even if the new treatments and therapies don't help. I can still create art. That's all that matters. I need to rest up now. Nurse Ratched will be here soon to do my physical therapy/torture."

My throat constricted, and I narrowed my eyes. "Do you want me to speak to your PT about easing up on you?"

Claire snorted. "No, my over-protective sister, absolutely not. Tell her to be harder on me. I want progress, and the PT at the assisted living home only came in once a week. I'm woefully behind where I should be."

"Very well. I'll tell her to turn the screws on you." I leaned over and kissed her temple.

"Thanks, Sis! I like your husband." Her hand came up awkwardly and patted my head. Sofia smiled at Claire's statement.

"Temporary husband," I said automatically, earning a frown from Sofia.

Sofia kissed Claire on the cheek, grabbed my hand, and said, "Today we put the final touches on decorating our boat for the Christmas on the Teche boat parade. Will you be able to come out and see the parade, Ms. Claire?"

"Not tonight. After physical therapy, I usually sleep until morning."

Sofia nodded, understanding. "I'll send you pictures, then."

"You do that, Sofia, and I'll show you pictures of my favorite outfits. I *will* convince you to switch to pastels."

Sofia squealed. Claire, before the accident, had a pastel gothic esthetic. I left them to debate Sofia's conversion to pastel goth.

"So, Ms. Claire thinks that I should add pastel goth to my outfits. She's going to show me pictures of herself. I think it is a good idea, because while I like black, I also like pink and I want a pink tutu and not just a black tutu. Do you think you could get me some white Doc Martens? Ms. Claire says you can take a metallic pastel sharpie and decorate them. Ms. Claire says that she's getting better at drawing with her mouth and I can hold the boots and she will draw on them. Don't you think that'll be cool, Daddy?"

Marc was busy hanging lights as Sofia chattered at him. I couldn't hide my grin.

"I see that Ms. Claire has made an impression on you." Marc kept his eyes on the lights, but his dimples were peeking out.

"She is *so* cool, Daddy. Not that you're not cool too, Ms. Kayleigh." She spun towards me and gave me a hug.

I kissed the top of her head and admitted, "I have never been, nor will I ever be, as cool as my sister."

"Sofia, why don't you go down and get a snack ready for us and read your book for a few minutes? That way, we'll finish decorating and you can come up with fresh eyes and give us your opinion."

"Sure thing, Daddy. That's a bunny day. Chef Agnès sent us some satsumas and watermelon, the rest of her sourdough *boule,* and some herbed goat cheese she made. Don't you think that'll be yummy? The cheese and the fresh herbs are from the *Mes Rêves* farm. Ms. Renee sent it to her. Wasn't that nice, Daddy?"

Marc pressed his lips together. Bunny day was what they said at Sofia's French Immersion school for good idea, because that's what it sounds like in French. "Super nice, and now you've made me hungry. Why don't you go and fix us each a plate? But first read a chapter of your book. I don't want you to get behind in your school reading."

Sofia grinned. "I'm not behind, Daddy. I've already read all the fourth grade books. I'm working on the fifth grade books. I'll read a chapter and then make you and Ms. Kayleigh a snack plate to share." She kissed his cheek and went below deck.

I exhaled loudly. "Wow! I'm exhausted. How do you keep up with her? She was always a pistol in the library, but this is a whole other level of exuberance."

"It's a team effort. Between myself, my staff, my parents, and the Krewe, we give her space to fly without her spinning out of control. Dancing at Gelly's school has helped. I don't know what I would do without *Danse avec moi*. Plus, she dances with her best friend, Bailey Marie. After dance class, Shell and Beau always take them to Myran's for dinner. A night with Bailey Marie, Tanner, Valerie, and little Alex usually wears her out and keeps her mellow for a couple of days."

I glanced up from the lightbulbs I was swapping out. "You're doing an amazing job with her. She's a sweet, wonderful child."

His dimples emerged, and a warmth ran through me as we finished decorating. After we scarfed down the snack Sofia had fixed for us, we lit the lights and strolled on the deck together to admire our handy work. At the bow of the boat, Marc had shaped the lights to form a giant Christmas tree with presents below it. In addition, on each side of the boat, he created two reindeer in full flight. With metal rails following behind the boat, was Santa's sleigh and Santa himself. Layered underneath the Santa lights were lights of snowmen, and for the grand finale, a Nativity scene.

"Woah! I can't wait to see y'all go by in the parade." Sofia gaped at that boat as we switched to test out the various visible lights.

"You aren't coming with us?" I asked.

Sofia shook her head. "I want to see all the boats. Plus, if Claire wakes up and wants to watch the boats, I don't want her to be alone."

"Besides," Marc added, "that's our usual ritual. She'll be with Mawmaw and Pawpaw Richard. Won't you, my little book dragon?" He turned to me. "You and I will navigate the boat."

I grinned, and not just because Marc had adopted my nickname for Sofia. "I've never been in a parade."

Marc side hugged me. "It'll be fun." *Famous last words.*

19

Christmas on the Bayou

Marc

The parade started out as a blast. The boats were in queue, all lit up with their Christmas decorations. A band played classic Cajun Christmas music on the stage constructed by the boat landing. Food vendors sold spicy Natchitoches-like meat pies, sweet, cinnamony sweet potato pies, and hot chocolate, both the virgin and spiked varieties. After sampling the food with Sofia and my parents and dancing to a couple of Christmas classics, we made our way through the festivities to the boat landing. As Kayleigh and I cruised down the Bayou Teche, my men discreetly followed behind us, out of sight from the onlookers, guarding my boat and, more importantly, guarding Kayleigh. My task tonight was to navigate the boat and Kayleigh's was to hit a button to toggle through the various light shows we created. The first light show was the snowman scene. When we had traveled a quarter of the way down the bayou, she switched to the Christmas tree lights. In front of the judges, she would light up Santa's sleigh, and as we finished the route, she would finish it up with the nativity scene.

With each scene, her eyes shone with amazement. I had held back some elements during our demonstration. I enjoyed adding that element of drama. Watching her unrestrained emotions, I couldn't help but reflect back on our night together. While we were halfway through the parade and alone together, I realized we needed to have a conversation about our next steps.

"Can we talk?" I asked her as the boat sailed easily down the bayou. The oohs and ahh's of the spectators were background noise.

Kayleigh rubbed her arms. "That's never good. What's wrong?"

"Are you cold?" I took off my jacket and held it out to her.

She smiled, reached for my jacket, and put it on. I could have sworn she took a sniff as she was putting it on.

"Did you just smell my jacket?"

"Shut up! I like your cologne, that's all." She threw the leftover paper wrapper from her meat pie at me.

I grinned and dodged, but kept the paper from going overboard.

"So, can we talk? I wanted to discuss the other night." I kept my eyes fixed on the Teche. Sometimes avoiding eye contact with her, just like one would do with a rabid bunny. was the safest path.

"Which night?" she hedged. Pretending she didn't know as she watched the lights on the other boats in the parade.

"Ouch."

She chuckled and turned back to me. "Oh, that night. Whatcha want to discuss?"

"I was thinking of adding to our relationship agreement." I turned to look at her. Expecting agreement and accordance. She was lovely, like a sexy Tinker Bell.

Kayleigh's eyes turned to flames. Distracted by lust, I missed the danger signals. "You want to add ... physical intimacy to a contract that outlines mutual benefits."

"Exactly."

Her voice softened and slowed. I thought it was a good sign. "I see, and what, exactly, would you add to the agreement so that we could include that physical intimacy?"

"Well, I was thinking I could increase the amount of money you get once you decide to leave the relationship. Perhaps even ensure Claire's care with my team of experts in perpetuity."

"I see. This all seems so familiar. So a carrot of more money, if I do what you want, which is to say, if I continue sleeping with you. And emotional blackmail, Claire losing her care, if I do not." She flipped the lights on cue, but with more energy than needed.

"That's not what I —"

"—No, no, I get it. You're just like Nonc Bill. Paying for what you want. Paying to try to control me." *Cue Rabid Bunny.*

"That wasn't what I wanted. I just wanted to make sure you benefited if we added intimacy to our relationship."

"Just what every girl wants, to feel like a prostitute." She flipped the lights again to the applause of the parade spectators.

As the lights transformed from a Christmas tree to Santa and his reindeer, I realized my mistake. "That's not what I meant. I just wanted you to know that I would always take care of you and Claire."

"Oh ... Yay! I get to be a kept woman. You sure this is the kind of relationship you want to model for Sofia? How would you feel if some guy told her he would pay her more to sleep with him?"

"That's not what I ... Okay, I might have done that, but I only wanted you to be protected."

"*Ça c'est de la merde.* Don't give me that B.S. You're protecting yourself. I never asked for your genuine emotions. I don't want what you don't want to give, but don't you dare malign me, or make me feel like your property. And, Marc—" She flipped one more switch for the big finale and the crowd went wild.

"Yes?"

As the nativity scene lit up the boat, rage lit Kayleigh's face. "*Piqué toi.*" With that, she pushed me overboard into the Bayou. She made sure my head resurfaced and threw me a life vest. "You really need to remember that how you treat women will be, how Sofia will expect to be treated. I, personally, will show her that you don't take gruff from any man."

My men who had been following behind us picked me up. Kayleigh docked the boat like I taught her and stormed towards my parents. She murmured a few words to Sofia before setting off on her own. My dad, bless him, caught her by the arm and directed her to Beau and Shell. She went off with them.

Dammit, why can't I talk to this woman? I texted the Krewe in a group text on my way to shore.

> Thanks, Beau, for making sure she's safe.

> Beau: I don't know what you did, bro, but even Shell is mad at you.

> I was just trying to move our relationship to the next level.

> Armand: How?

> By adjusting the relationship agreement. Like I usually do.

The three dots showed someone was trying to respond. No one commented, so I added:

> That's how I always move forward. It protects both parties.

Etienne: I don't understand. What's the next level?

Sex

More dots, and radio silence followed. Then Armand responded.

Armand: You want my cousin to sign an agreement outlining the benefits of … I'm sorry, Marc, I'm going to have to beat your *tchu*.

That's what I always do in all my relationships.

Armand: You will not treat my cousin like that!

Etienne: You're an idiot.

Beau: Marc, that might have worked with your gold diggers, but Kayleigh's different. It's disrespectful. You better hope no one ever treats Sofia like that.

Right after that, a text came in from Kayleigh.

Kayleigh: I'm staying at Beau and Shell's tonight. Please don't kick my sister onto the street because I'm not going to sleep with you. Good night.

I would never do that.

Three dots again and then nothing. Finally, a text from my mom popped up.

> Mom: We are taking Sofia home. She's not happy that you made Kayleigh mad again. I'm not happy either. She was smiling when she got on your boat. Now she's in tears, but putting on a brave face. What did you do? No, don't tell me. Just fix it!

When I got home, my parents, Sofia, and Claire were all giving me the silent treatment.

I used to think myself adept with women. Apparently, they were different types of women. My evening did not improve when my phone rang. It was Ms. Clothilde, sticking her nose in where it did not belong.

"Good evening, Marc."

"Good evening, Ms. Clothilde. How can I help you tonight?"

"Well, I have a nephew, Reggie Landry. Do you know him?"

"Sure, he's close with Etienne."

"They are cousins, but who isn't in Meauxville? Now I don't want to stick my nose in where it doesn't belong."

I rolled my eyes at that whopper. "I'm sure. How can I help you, Ms. Clothilde?"

"Well, word on the street is that you and Kayleigh plan to annul your marriage. Like it never even happened. Reggie just wanted to know when you were thinking of doing that."

Frowning at my phone in confusion, I asked, "I'm sorry. Who says I'm getting an annulment?"

"Why, nearly everyone I speak to. Plus, there was the boat parade incident. When Kayleigh pushed you overboard, that seemed to confirm the whole getting an annulment story."

"Well, I'm not! You can tell Reggie to look elsewhere. Kayleigh is not, nor will she ever be, 'back on the market.'"

"Alright, don't kill the messenger. Kayleigh is such a sweet, hardworking girl. Always taking care of her sister. If it were up to her worthless parents, neither of the girls would have survived. She's just the kind of girl I would love for Reggie to date."

"Well, he can't date her. Let him know."

"Don't get your panties in a bunch. I'll let you get to bed. Based on Kayleigh's face when she left the boat parade, you are gonna need some restorative rest and a bushel of 'I'm sorry' flowers. You'll let me know if she decides to stop putting up with your foolishness, won't you?"

Grinding my teeth, I was able to say, "Have a pleasant night, Mrs. Clothilde."

"*Bonne nuit,* Marc," she said, and I could've sworn I heard cackling before I hung up the phone.

Today was a cluster. I grabbed my Lagavulin bottle and headed to bed. At least Kayleigh was safe at Beau's.

20

Betrayal

Kayleigh

I began my work day early today. The routine and the smell of old books centered me after yesterday's betrayal. Christmas was the season of giving, but I'd be damned if I gave my favors for reciprocal benefits. See, that's why I avoided relationships. It was just give and take. *And all I ever do is give.* With a growl, I focused on finishing up the library's final Christmas decorations. Once Christmas decorations were in place, I chose my stories for the remaining two holiday story times: *Polar Express, Gingerbread Baby,* and *A Cranberry Christmas.* The phone rang as I sat down with my first cup of tea to practice reading my selections.

"Good morning, Breaux Bridge Library. How can I help you?"

"Ms. Breaux. This is Paul Boudreaux. I'm Mr. Richard's head of security. I needed to let you know that your sister, Claire, was in an accident."

I set my books aside and rose abruptly from the chair. "How? She's safe at Marc's house."

"She ... uh ... fell off the bed during physical therapy."

I blinked, confused. "The physical therapist did the therapy on her bed? The therapist has always worked in Marc's gym."

Paul sounded annoyed. "He did this time."

"Is she OK?" I grabbed my purse, searching for my keys in case I needed to lock up the library.

"We took her to the hospital."

"Why didn't you lead with that? Where? Which hospital? Hold on." I switched to speakerphone, ready to order an Uber.

"Our Lady. I sent a car to pick you up. I'll wait for you and bring you to her room."

With a release of breath, I relaxed. I would see Claire soon. "I'll be waiting outside the library."

While I was waiting for the car to pick me up, I locked the library and texted my boss. Then I texted Marc.

> Why didn't you tell me Claire was injured? Why have your lackey tell me?

Marc didn't respond. The car and driver pulled up shortly thereafter. Paul jumped out and opened the door for me. I recognized him from Marc's house. As soon as I entered the car, I realized my mistake. Paul, the traitor, followed me in, securing my arm. Seated in the far corner, grinning like a cat with cream, was none other than Nonc Bill. I made to escape, but Paul had my arm in a vice grip and I heard the car locks click into place.

"No way out, my wayward niece." Nonc Bill's malevolent smirk did not bode well for me.

I did not fold. If this was a ruse, that meant that Claire was safe. I breathed a sigh of relief. That's what mattered. Marc would keep Claire safe, and that was my only concern. So my uncle could just get screwed. I smiled sweetly and lashed out at him. "Aren't you supposed to be in jail somewhere making some big bad man an old, old lady?"

He slapped my face, and I just smirked. "I'm out on bond. I'm a respected member of society. Sheriff Trahan's investigation isn't going anywhere and the Sheriff will face a tough battle in his next election to stay in office."

As I stared out the window, I tapped the record icon on my watch, hoping they would not remember to get rid of my phone. A little trick I learned from Shell.

"I don't know what you think you are doing. Marc will come, with his security force, at least the loyal ones." Turning back to them, my eyes narrowed on Paul the traitor. He looked away. *Good. Feel guilty.*

"Your fake husband will not look for you. Paul already left him a note that practically mirrored the note that his dear Tracy had left him when she ran off with his cousin. Which means that your sister will be out on the street soon and will need my protection. I'm not a terrible protector. Your father enjoys not having to worry about funds."

"What's your plan here, Nonc Bill? You think your actions will be forgiven?" I turned toward the window, tracking our progress and noting landmarks.

"I need you to sign over your and Claire's portion of your inheritance to me."

I chuckled. "That's not how inheritances work. I don't get anything until you and my dad die. Also, Hercule Trahan explained that you don't actually have legal right to the money. Even the money my father signed over to you isn't legally yours. You're in control only because he allows you to be. I don't think I want to know what you hold over him to get that control, but he seems content, so I have no issues with that. Why don't you just enjoy your money while it's under your control?"

"Control of fortunes should go to the first-born son of the first-born son," he said as the car pulled up to a generic, cheap motel in Lafayette. I didn't even see the name.

Antagonizing people was part of my genetic makeup, so I couldn't resist saying, "So, my cousin Armand?"

Nonc Bill slapped me again, harder this time. "Legitimate children, not bastards." Then he got out and dragged me with him.

My cheek smarted, but if I was going out, it'd be in a blaze of glory. "Wow, how very eighteenth century of you. Do you have other aristocratic tendencies as well? You know, like inter-breeding and syphilis." That earned a hard tug into the motel room.

"Of course you refuse to be reasonable. When have you ever been reasonable? My brother should've taken a strap to you. I told him often enough. Tie her to the chair."

Marc will come! With an inhale to calm my jagged nerves, I repeated that mantra in my head as Paul, the traitor, bound me to the chair.

I pulled against the ropes binding my hands and feet. There was no give. "Again I ask, what's your plan here, Nonc Bill? You can't legally get my inheritance."

"Like you said, I'm an old-fashioned guy, so I'm going to get it the old-fashioned way. I'm going to have you committed and then take over your fortune."

He nodded to a man lurking in the corner. He had on scrubs, but he looked dirty and hard-worn. The needle he took out of his satchel looked bright and shiny, though.

I swallowed my nerves. "From jail? You think a judge will give a criminal that kind of control?"

"That investigation will be over soon. I have a DA who owes me a favor. Plus, I've already spoken to a distant nephew about replacing Sheriff Trahan. This investigation is about to go away." He nodded to the doctor, who came towards me.

In for a penny. I raised my eyebrows innocently. "Really, which DA and which one of my distant cousins?"

Nonc Bill paused at that. He wasn't stupid.

"Paul, you moron. You took her phone off of her, right?"

Paul shook his head. "You never said anything about a phone. I did what you told me to do to keep my grandpa safe."

I tsked at my uncle. "Blackmailing the help is not the way to get loyal minions, Billy." He punched me in the face this time and it split my lip. I ran my tongue over my teeth, relieved that they were all intact. I shook my head to stop the ringing in my ears. "See, Paul, if you helped me, I bet Marc would go easy on you. I mean, being a snitch is one thing; kidnapping, that's a whole new level of diabolical. Also, it moves it to a federal crime. Are you an evil person, Paul? I bet he doesn't have the pull you think he does."

"I do, and if he makes one wrong move, I have a gal at the home who can easily get rid of his grandfather."

I blinked my sweet eyes at him. "Really? Who?"

"God dammit." Nonc Bill moved to me, frisked me, took my phone, and stomped on it.

"Good thing there is no cloud of information to which the recording would be uploaded. Too bad you smashed my phone or you could have gotten me to delete whatever was saved on my cloud. See, Paul. Now it is on record that he's threatening your grandpa's life. I'm sure Marc would understand. If, and only if, you help me out of this little jam."

"He can't help you. His hands are too dirty." Nonc Bill turned to me. "Now shut your mouth, or I will get my *friends* to go on a rampage. You'll die first ... brutally, then your sister. I'll make it look like an accident. After that, I'll make sure that your little Sofia is taken care of as well." He turned to the doctor. "Drug her now!"

"You hurt Sofia or Claire, and I will either kill you now or haunt you forever." Then I turned to Paul. Hesitation showed in his eyes. As the 'doctor' came forward to give me a shot. Paul's hand reached out and stopped him.

"Boy, this is a mistake." Bill took out his phone and said, "One phone call and your grandfather won't survive."

Paul hit the phone out of his hand. Bill immediately reached for his gun from behind his back and pointed it at me. "At least Brandon will get your share of the money." When Bill's gun went off, Paul leaped in front of me as Marc broke down the door.

21

Not Betrayal

Marc

Where the hell was Kayleigh? As Sofia danced around Claire's room, getting ready for her last dance rehearsal before the recital, Kayleigh was nowhere to be found. Sofia wasn't worried. There was no doubt in her mind Kayleigh would honor her promise to attend the recital; it wasn't in her nature to break her word. But I assumed she'd show up for the rehearsal as well. She'd gone to every other rehearsal with Sofia. A sense of unease washed over me. I checked Kayleigh's room and found a letter on her made bed with my name written on it.

I grabbed the letter and headed to the surveillance room. My video tech backed the video up to when Kayleigh left as I read the letter. The words hit hard, but they didn't sound like Kayleigh. I shook my head. Something was off. The camera placed in the hall, not her room, showed her unmade bed as she left the day before. Only the maid entered her room after that. Then the video feed on that particular camera malfunctioned. Someone placed the letter on her bed after the maid left. *I'm being played.* My fists clenched and I couldn't shake the dread. I checked my phone.

> Kayleigh: Why didn't you tell me Claire was injured? Why have your lackey tell me?

I ran to Claire's room and asked, "Did you see Kayleigh today?"

"She called me this morning before work." Claire said, glugging her post PT energy drink.

This is what happens when you get cocky. I thought I could keep Paul in check and use him. He had to be the lackey that Kayleigh spoke with. I re-scanned the note and saw the resemblance. Kayleigh would never have written this letter. If she left, she'd go out punching. No, this letter was nearly identical to Tracy's. My instincts were correct; this was a setup.

I crumpled the letter in my hand and ran to Sofia's room. "Did Kaleigh say she was going to Lafayette or somewhere else out-of-town today?"

Sofia shrugged. "No, her plans were to go to the library and then head here to ride with me to rehearsal. Is something wrong?"

"Yes, no, maybe. I have to go." I looked over to Sofia, "Sofia darlin', only the Krewe takes you anywhere."

Sofia tensed. "What's wrong, Daddy?"

"I'm going to find out. Only the Krewe. Promise me."

"I promise."

"I'll keep an eye on her," Claire told me as she rolled into the room, her eyes meeting mine, and her hand holding Sofia's shoulder.

With a nod, I headed out, calling the Krewe on speaker. I did not wait for greetings. "Beau, I need you and Shell to pick up Sofia and take her to the recital. Do not leave any of the *Littles* alone at all. Armand, I want someone behind the scene as well."

Beau said, "I'm heading to pick her up now."

While Armand said, "That was already my plan. What's going on?"

Bringing up the Find My phone app, I searched for Kayleigh's phone. I'd ask for forgiveness later for adding it to her phone without permission. The app showed her phone to be on the outskirts of Lafayette. I pulled up her cloud file. She had a recording happening in real time. *That's my girl.*

Armand repeated, "What is going on, Marc?"

Focused on the mission, I didn't answer him directly. "Etienne, I'm sending you a link to a recording that is occurring now. I need you to get on and listen and let me know if I need to know anything. I think Kayleigh's been kidnapped."

Etienne swore and then added, "I'm calling Bradley. This needs to end now."

I zoomed in on Kayleigh's location in the Find My app. She was at an old motel on the outskirts of Lafayette. That note flashed again in my mind, but it did not fit with Kayleigh. She and Tracy had nothing in common. She didn't sleep around. I knew that for a fact. I started my car and punched the accelerator. A speeding ticket meant nothing. Kayleigh was ... important. I gave the Krewe my destination and then clicked my phone off. *C'mon Kayleigh, I'm nearly there. Stay alive.*

My men followed me in their SUVs. We pulled up to the hotel and spotted some armed men huddled outside a room. *At least I don't have to search for her.* We surrounded them, and they surrendered immediately. I could hear commotion through the door.

"You hurt Sofia or Claire and I will either kill you now or haunt you forever." *Kayleigh's voice.*

"Boy, this is a mistake. One phone call and your grandfather won't survive. At least Brandon will get your share of the money." *Her uncle's voice,* and that was the last thing I processed before we broke through the door. Everything blurred, but I focused on Bill, the threat. My gun fired as Bill's blasted. I rushed to Kayleigh, but Paul was huddled in front of her. I grabbed to pull him off of her.

"No! Don't hurt him." Kayleigh said, "He saved me. You need to get him medical help and protect his grandpa."

My men were already calling for an ambulance and had that bastard Bill in zip ties, injury or no. We tied up all of Bill's men, including his crooked doctor. I listened to the recording that my quick-thinking Kayleigh had made, while my medic looked her over for injuries. She had been cleared to go when Bradley Trahan, our local sheriff, drove up.

Sheriff Trahan got down from his SUV, sauntered up to me, and heaved a sigh. "Marc, you're not the law. This is not your jurisdiction. This isn't even my jurisdiction."

"I know. I'm just serving as an intermediary until the Lafayette Parish Sheriff's department arrives. By the way, Etienne texted and sent me an interesting recording. Apparently, we have a dirty DA."

Bill stood tall, ignoring his shoulder injury. "You are soon to lose your job, Sheriff."

Bradley held up his finger for silence and listened to the recording. He grinned at Bill. "What a fascinating recording, Bill. Apparently, you're setting up a family member who'll take my place and do your bidding. Kayleigh, sweetie, can I have a copy for my re-election campaign?"

"Absolutely!" She grinned at Bradley, and my eyes narrowed. I flung a possessive arm around her and pulled her close.

Bradley smirked at me and went to speak with the Lafayette Parish Sheriff's Deputies, who had just arrived on the scene. Sheriff Bradley was very helpful. He forwarded a copy of the audio to them that Etienne had sent from his official FBI account. "Tell the Sheriff, we can root out the crooked DA together and run our re-election campaigns on anti-corruption."

The Lafayette EMTs lifted Paul onto a gurney. Paul grunted. "I'm sorry, boss."

"You should be. But since you saved Kayleigh, I'll make sure your grandfather is safe. I don't know if I can help you, but I'll see what I can do. And Paul ..."

With a single nod, Paul indicated his agreement and understanding.

"Is there anyone else?"

Paul shook his head and winced in pain. "No, he didn't need anyone else. He had me."

I nodded and told the EMTs to take him away.

Kayleigh sat on the curb outside the hotel, resting. I moved to her and picked her up. She was so slight, so small.

"What are you doing?" she asked. She sounded annoyed, but she laid her head on my shoulder.

"Just making sure you're safe. I may have to handcuff you to me." Laying my cheek against her hair, I inhaled lavender and cinnamon and kissed her temple.

With a shiver, she repeated, "Handcuffs," under her breath and licked her lips.

My grip tightened on her. That's a notion for a different time. "So, you planned to haunt your uncle." I smiled and set her in the back of my SUV.

"Hey, I had to play with the cards I was dealt. You were taking your sweet time finding me. Probably didn't even notice I'd been kidnapped. Hence the recording and the threat of a haunting."

"Thanks for protecting Sofia and Claire." I kissed her cheek.

"I'm a librarian protecting children is our prime directive. To tell the truth, I don't think my threat to haunt him proved all that effective." She frowned at my snort. "Rude. Changing the subject, how did you find me? I thought for sure I was a goner. My long shot rescue plan entailed guilting Paul into not being a complete douche."

"It worked."

"And yet, not an answer to my question. Don't get me wrong, I'm ecstatic you're here. How did you find me?"

Scratching my chin, I averted my gaze and readied myself for the explosion. "I might have added your phone to my phone plan and used the Find My app."

Kayleigh nodded. "Later, I'll be pissed at your high-handed tactics. For now, I'll say 'thank you.'" With that, she gave me an avuncular kiss on the cheek. *Not the best reaction, but not the worst either.*

22

Dance Recital

Kayleigh

We had missed rehearsal, due to the aforementioned kidnapping. I made Marc stop by the house to reassure Claire that I was fine and to change into nicer clothes. When we got to the *Dance avec moi* dance studio, the dancers were getting into their costumes. The dressing room was awash in tutus and glitter. Sofia was sitting on a bench in the dressing room debating tutus.

I ran over to her and hugged her. "Hey *Chérie*, I'm sorry I missed your rehearsal."

"Are you alright? Daddy and Ms. Claire were worried about you. I was worried, too." She hugged me back, and I was awash in the smell of sugar cookies and Downy.

"I'm fine. Your daddy took care of everything." Sofia nodded, acknowledging that inevitable fact. In her world, Marc did take care of all of her problems. Although she was frowning, so maybe not every problem.

I brushed her bangs back. "What's wrong, Sof?"

"I can't choose. We get our choice of tutu colors for the performance, either black or pink. I've always worn black because I love Abbie Sciutto on *NCIS*."

I grinned at that. "So, what's the issue?"

"Well, Ms. Claire was showing me pictures of her pastel goth outfits. The colors are so pretty and pink is one of those colors. So, I like that too." Sofia laid her head on my shoulder as she showed me an old picture of Claire with her hair dyed a vibrant pink and periwinkle. She wore pink and black striped tights, and a pleated plaid mini skirt with coordinating pink and black hues. I had forgotten how adorable my pastel goth sister had been. I guffawed, but coughed to cover it up.

I straightened my face. "A dilemma." I tapped my finger on my chin. "Hold on. What exactly were you told about the tutus?"

"Ms. Gelly said we had to choose from black tutus and pink tutus. No other colors."

The corner of my mouth curved up. "And she used the word *and*?"

Sofia's head came up at that statement and she reflected. "Yes, even in French dance class. She said, *les tutus noirs **et** les tutus roses.*"

I shook out the pink tutu. "In that case, you don't need to choose. Can you dance with both tutus on?"

"Yes! I can dance with 10 tutus on. I've tried it," she said and put on both her tutus.

No doubt you have. With a grin and a wink, I turned to leave the dressing room. "Break a leg, sweetie!"

Sofia cocked her and said, "We need to look up why people say that."

"We'll just ask Claire. She'll know." Sofia nodded and finished dressing as I made my way to the door.

Marc was leaning against the doorframe, his arms crossed over his chest. His eyes focused on Sofia prancing around in her double tutus.

"You are a pain in my *tchu,* but you raised an amazing girl. I love that kid!" I told him, kissed his cheek, and then beat a retreat out the dressing room door. I glanced over my shoulder and asked, "Did I thank you for rescuing me?"

He followed me out the door. "You had already sweet-talked Paul into helping you before I got there."

"It still could have turned out worse if you hadn't arrived." I took my seat in the audience.

Marc sat beside me. "I tell you what, we'll be even steven, if you promise to always wear the outerwear I bought for you."

"The Kevlar jackets and vests? That's just insane." I rolled my eyes.

"Even steven, I can't hold anything over your head. Plus, I can't tell you how right I was for taking over your phone account and adding it to mine." Marc grinned.

"Heavy handed," I whispered.

"Saved some lives. Also, if you do this one thing for me, I will never again mention how much better your life is under my roof."

I turned to him. "You're a control freak."

"And you can control my mouth. In this, and other things." He mumbled that last part, but warmth spread through my body when he said that.

I cleared my throat. "I wear your stupid outerwear, for no reason, because they have Nonc Bill in custody, and you keep your big trap shut? That's the deal?"

He nodded. "That's the deal."

"Great, I'll start tomorrow." I turned back to scan the dance floor. Sofia was on her mark and prepared to begin.

"You'll start tonight." He lifted his chin to signal one of his men. That man brought over a bright red fleece vest.

I tapped my foot. He was infuriating. "Fine, but only because it's cute and happens to match my outfit."

Marc nodded and tapped away on his phone. *Why do I think I'll have a vest in every color when I get back home?* Then three *coups* [taps with a stick] sounded and the Christmas recital began. Gelly took the mic and thanked the parents and grandparents, aunts, uncles, nannies, and *parrains* for supporting her dancers. Our friends sat beside us in the staggered seating area as we watched the dancing. Sofia was so talented. Every time she did a pirouette or jumped, I turned to Marc, and he smiled down at me. I grabbed his hand and squeezed. Sometimes, he wasn't a complete jerk.

After the recital, we were having milkshakes at Myran's when Marc's phone rang.

"Yeah? ... Who? ... Do we have eyes on him? ... Okay, we're heading back." Conversations at the adult table had stopped. "We need to head back. A DA pretended Bill was being transferred and then let him free."

"Which DA?" Etienne asked, forever in lawman mode and pulling out his phone to text his bosses at the FBI. Corrupt state officials was their domain.

"Robert Thibodeaux. Apparently, they found some explicit texts to underage girls on his phone when they raided his home. They think Bill was blackmailing him."

Etienne looked up from his text. "They already have him in custody?" Marc nodded and Etienne passed that information along.

"Hell is not hot enough for people like that." Shell said. As a school principal, she was a fervent protector of children.

"True dat!" Renee, another educator, said. "May he rot in hell."

Grabbing Marc's hand under the table, I squeezed it, needing reassurance.

He scanned the restaurant and then focused on the *Littles* at their kid's table. Laughing and having fun, except for Valerie, the oldest one. She could sense danger. "We need to move to a more secure location. Why don't y'all come to my place? The kids can play in the playroom under the watchful eyes of the au pair and my guards, and we can relax while my men work to find Bill."

We gathered up the *Littles* and headed for our house — I meant, Marc's home. Renee's parents met us there with the twins. As Nonc Bill's grandchildren by blood, they too were at risk. The tension in my neck and shoulders released as soon as we got the children in the playroom with the guards surrounding them.

Once the *Littles* were situated, we all met in the family room.

"Time for some libations," Marc said. He walked over to the decanter tray and poured each of us a finger of peaty, dark scotch.

"Here, here," I seconded, reaching for a glass. "It is not every day you get kidnapped."

At that, Armand came over and gave me a hug. "I'm glad you're alright, Cuz."

"Alright, she was fearsome. You should have heard her on the recording. Snapping at Useless Bill, calling him names, and threatening to haunt him if he killed her," Marc bragged.

At that I broke down into tears, for no reason, like a weakling. Marc peeled me away from Armand, who was awkwardly patting me on the back. Marc picked me up and moved me to his lap on his recliner and started rocking.

"It's over. You don't have to worry anymore." He handed me a clean handkerchief.

I shook my head. "Clearly it's not over. That's why everyone is over here. Nonc Bill is still out there and now he has nothing to lose." Marc rocked and held me close, but I could feel him nodding his head. The next morning, I woke up tucked into bed fully dressed except for my shoes. My eyes scanned my room. *We're safe ... for now.*

23

Cajun Night Before Christmas Party

Marc

Our *Cajun Night Before Christmas* party was supposed to be on the Babineaux complex. But nearly everyone was already at my place, so we just switched the venue. This afternoon, the grandparents would arrive to lend a hand in the kitchen and distribute presents. This morning, we were all meeting for a Christmas breakfast.

When Kayleigh walked in, she resembled an adorable elf in her green jeans, plaid turtleneck, and the red fleece kevlar vest I had gifted her. I nodded at the vest. All the *Littles* rushed in at once. It wasn't Christmas, but they knew they would get one present to open before the reading of the *Cajun Night Before Christmas*. Kayleigh and Sofia started on *Papa Noël*-shaped pancakes. Kayleigh sculpted the pancake to resemble Santa, while Sofia giggled and squirted whipped cream for the beard and fluffy hat. The Krewe set the table and distributed the *Papa Noël* pancakes along with juice, coffee, and a variety of syrups.

"*Viens manger!*" Sofia yelled to get everyone to the table.

"*Venez manger.*" Shell winked at Sofia and gave her the plural version of come and eat. While the pancakes tasted sweet and fluffy, we ate our meal in near silence. Our thoughts churned with ideas about how we could make sure the *Littles* remained safe. Until the end when Sofia came forward representing the *Littles* delegation and brought our thoughts to the present moment.

"Daddy," Sofia asked. "When can we open our books?"

The tradition started when Shell came into the group. Reading was a top priority for her as a principal. We already had our tradition of reading the *Cajun Night Before Christmas* a few days before Christmas eve, and she added the tradition of buying a book for each child. A simple task because, years before, Kayleigh had started a library program where parents could ask for book recommendations based on the books their children checked out. This year, I hadn't even worried about the book. Kayleigh had purchased it when she and Sofia did their Black Friday shopping.

"We will open the presents after we eat dinner," I told her.

"Dinner lunch or dinner supper?"

I grinned because she caught my trick. "Dinner lunch. Does that work for you? Now go and watch your Christmas movie extravaganza marathon."

The *Littles* tramped out of the dining room until Renee let out a shrill whistle. She, Shell, and Kayleigh raised their eyebrows and crossed their arms. With heavy sighs, the children dutifully cleared their plates from the table and scraped their leftovers into the compost bin before placing them in the sink. Then off they ran.

"I need to learn that eyebrow trick," Armand said.

"It won't work on ours yet or little Ellie. Speaking of which, the Morlocks need some sustenance, so you get to help with kitchen duty." Renee walked off to nurse Amelie and Blaise.

Armand started clearing off the table. "I swear she's in league with the Morlocks. Anytime there is a chore or task Renee wants to avoid, they get hungry. It's a conspiracy." But he grinned as he cleared the table.

Kayleigh patted Armand's shoulder in sympathy. "*Pauvre bête*. See ya!"

"Where are you headed? You don't have the 'twins' excuse, Cuz," Armand said.

Kayleigh rolled her eyes. "I cook, you clean. Besides, I'm the reader and I need to practice for the read-aloud tonight. I have character voices that I need to solidify. It's not just reading, you know." Taking on an English accent, she added, "There is theatre involved." She grabbed Shell's hand to enlist her and give her a lead-up book to read before the big *Cajun Night Before Christmas* finale. Armand, Beau, and I ended up with clean up duty. I'd have delegated the task to my staff, but they were on holiday except for the protection detail.

After breakfast, the Krewe broke into two teams and began cooking either seafood or chicken and sausage gumbos. The competition sparked a fierce rivalry to decide which gumbo reigned supreme. As we finished up the gumbos, the grandparents arrived laden with sides and desserts. They put their potato salad, coleslaw, and deviled eggs on the sides table and the blueberry and banana, pecan, and sweet potato pies on the dessert table. As soon as the Hitachi rice cookers dinged, the kids made their way outside for the food. We were all seated, the kids at their table and the adults at theirs, when I tapped my beer with a gumbo spoon to get everyone's attention.

Looking over at Claire, who nodded at me, I began. "Everyone here knows that Kayleigh and I are legally married."

"Although how that happened when I was in a coma, I don't know." Kayleigh added, much to the amusement of my friends and family.

"Yes, well, money talks. What I wanted to say today was the fact that Kayleigh living here has been a blessing—"

"—Because I keep putting him in his place." My Kayleigh was on a roll.

"Yes, between Sofia, Claire, Kayleigh, and my mom, I'm outnumbered and outmaneuvered. But I have to say that I've come to enjoy that." Kayleigh snorted and kissed my cheek. "It is in hopes of continuing that struggle between what I think is right and what Kayleigh knows is right that I ask her this question." I kneeled in front of her and held up my engagement present to her. "Kayleigh Isabelle Breaux, will you marry me?"

Her eyes widened as she looked at the wrapped present that I offered to her, curiosity clear in her expression. She reached for the present.

As soon as she held it in her hands, she figured out what I gifted her. "You got me a book as an engagement gift?"

"I did. I already bought you a ring, so I wanted you to have something special. How about you don't leave me hanging?"

She raised her hand. "Hold on. I have to see which book it is before I answer." She unwrapped it, shredding through the paper. "*Oh, mon Dieu*! Oh, my God! It's a first edition of *Wuthering Heights*." She held the book to her and started jumping for joy.

"Uh ... Kayleigh?" I was still kneeling on the ground.

She rolled her eyes. "What? Oh!" And she lifted me up and then kissed me until I felt only her and heard only our heartbeats. Everyone at both tables clapped, and Sofia ran towards us to give us a hug. As we hugged, the sound of a single clap echoed through the air, lingering.

I turned my head and reached behind my back as Kayleigh stepped in front of Sofia. Bill Breaux stood there, gun trained on Kayleigh. In my peripheral vision, I saw the popped trunk. He must have hidden in my parents' car. Security didn't check the cars of family members. Thoughts raced through my mind, questioning if more gunmen lurked in the surrounding trunks.

"Now, I understand. I have nowhere to go, and I realize I won't make it out of here alive. I just want to ensure I take some of you with me. The more unworthy offspring I kill, the more my boy inherits. Starting with you, little girl. You never were easy. That's why I tried to get rid of you and your embarrassing sister in that accident. It's hard to find good help, so sometimes you have to take matters into your own hands. For the rest of you, I want y'all to see your children die. My son will inherit. He won't be blamed for my deeds, and that's all I wanted, anyway. Illegitimate brats don't deserve the money." He trained his gun on Armand, then thought better, and moved to Tanner.

Kayleigh, either to distract him or driven by rage, retorted, "Your actions were illegitimate, and there are no illegitimate children, only illegitimate parents. And based on your parenting thus far...you're an atrocious parent, Nonc Bill."

She pulled his attention enough for the Krewe to get their weapons.

"Too late for you," he told her. Gun trained on her, he aimed.

She smiled. "No, it is too late for you. Bye-bye Nonc Billy," because she knew that nickname enraged him and would focus his rage on her.

As we fired our guns, he managed to fire off one shot, and Kayleigh crumpled to the ground.

"Mama!" Sofia cried.

$$24$$

Hero

Kayleigh

I awoke in a familiar place to the sound of Mariah Carey's "All I Want for Christmas." What was it about that song? They played it on repeat. I was in that Southern Living hospital room again. That is to say, my room. Complete with both a lavender and a cinnamon candle burning. Once again, I took an inventory of my brain and body. *Hello, can I understand me?* English ... check. *Et asteur Il faut essayer mon français.* French ... check. All of my appendages worked, but my chest felt like a truck had rolled over it.

Nurse One walked in, smiling at me. "How're you doing? Can I get you some ice water?"

"Yes?" I wasn't sure which question I answered, but she handed me a cup with a straw and held it as I sipped the cool, refreshing water.

"Thank you."

She nodded. "Any pain?"

I nodded, and she adjusted my I.V.

My tense muscles loosened. "Thanks."

The nurse nodded again. "I'm going to go find Mr. Richard to let him know you're awake."

Within five minutes, Marc rushed in and advanced straight towards me.

At that moment, it all came back in a rush. "Sofia!" I bolted out of the bed like it was on fire. That was a regrettable decision. The pain radiated from my chest, taking my breath away. I closed my eyes, trying to ignore the pain and calm my breathing.

Marc put a comforting arm around my shoulder as he helped me lie back in bed. "Sofia's fine. You stepped in front of her and protected her." He leaned over me and pressed his lips to mine. He gave my lower lip a nip before he pulled away and frowned. "I'd take it as a personal favor if you could please stop getting hurt."

I rolled my eyes at him, ignoring the scent of Irish Spring that was clouding my thoughts. "If I wouldn't have gotten hurt, Sofia might have. Are you saying don't save Sofia?"

"Of course not. First, you wouldn't listen to me if I told you that, anyway. You rarely listen to me. Thank you, by the way." He kissed me again, this time lingering.

Smiling when we came up for oxygen, I said, "That's more like it. You're welcome. Also, if I don't listen to you, it's probably because you're being a *tchu*. Stop being a *tchu,* and I'll listen to you." A giggle erupted from the doorway and my smile widened. Sofia was all-knowing for a reason.

Marc huffed out a breath. "Sofia. *Chérie.* Can we have some privacy?"

Sofia peeked her head through the doorway. She had her goth Pippi Longstocking braids, but the ends were hot pink. Claire's plan to transform her into a pastel goth was in play. With a doubtful expression, she scolded her father. "I don't know Daddy. When you try to apologize to Kayleigh, sometimes you both end up yelling."

With a snort, I nodded. "So true. I'm glad I'm not the only one who notices."

Sofia snorted, as well, my mini-me. I grinned at Marc, because I was sure he heard the similarity.

Marc cupped the back of his head with his hand. "Sofia please."

"Fine! But don't mess this up!" Sofia ran in, kissed me on the cheek, hugged her daddy and skipped away.

I chuckled as Marc paced the room. "Well. I'm waiting."

He cleared his throat. "You don't let up, do you? Can't you take a simple thank you?"

"Can't you say a proper thank you?" I retorted.

Marc grinned and moved over to me then. He kissed my lips. "Thanks." He kissed me deeper. "For." This time, his hands framed my face as he kissed me again. "Thanks for saving Sofia." Our eyes met and his gaze seared into mine. As Marc's mouth descended to cover mine, my heart rate became erratic, causing the monitor to emit warning beeps. His fingers combed through my hair and he gripped my head, bringing me closer for a crushing kiss. A kiss that sent delicious shivers through my body and sent the heart rate monitor into overdrive.

Nurse One rushed into the room, responding to the incessant beeping. "Oh, sorry!" Upon entering, she comically pivoted, attempting to divert her gaze from us as she rushed out.

We broke apart then, grinning. Those damn dimples made their appearance again. I softened, marginally. "In all honesty, I love that little girl. I'll always protect Sofia, just like I'll always protect Claire." Then I beamed at him and it all came back to me. "Hey! You asked me to marry you."

He played with my hair and chuckled. "I did."

"With no relationship agreement or signed contract or NDA or anything?" I took his hand from my head and kissed it.

"Yep, and I will note while you kissed me after I asked, which I took for an implicit 'yes,' you never did verbally acknowledge that you wanted to marry me—"

"—I was interrupted by a maniac. However, just so you know, my answer is—"

"—No, don't answer now. They have you on pain meds for the deep bruising in your chest. Besides, this is not the proposal story I want to tell our grandkids."

"So controlling. Fine, we can wait." I leaned back and pain radiated through my chest. "I can't believe that little vest could stop a bullet."

Marc grimaced. "It wasn't the vest alone." With a sigh, he extended his arm towards the side table next to me and retrieved the tattered remains of my treasured first edition of *Wuthering Heights*.

"No!" My teeth ground together, and heat flashed through my body, and not in a good way. The heart monitor again went into overdrive. With my face in my hands, I worked on controlling my breathing. The pain of the deep breaths did nothing to abate my rage. "That *fils d'putain* destroyed my book! That was a first edition. Do you comprehend how hard it is to find a first edition? Of course you do, you found it for me. It was the best gift I ever received. I can't believe Nonc Bill destroyed it."

"He won't be destroying anything else. He's gone Kayleigh." With gentle movements, Marc traced soft circles on my shoulder to soothe my tension.

Nothing distracted or diverted me. "But it was a first edition," I moaned. "Also, it was the book you gave me when you proposed. Really proposed, not that relationship agreement re-negotiation BS that you tried to do earlier."

"Yes, I'm *couillon, couillon,* but I promise to find you a replacement book." He kissed my cheek as his hand squeezed mine.

"You were, but you *are* getting better. Sofia, Claire, and I will whip you into shape in no time. Also, I would love a new first edition, but I'm keeping this one as well." I closed my eyes and used my cheek to caress his hand.

His dimples flashed, for a moment, then large and in charge Marc came back to the fore. "You'll rest up today. Tomorrow they will have the reading of Bill's will. His widow is not having a wake or a ceremony. They just cremated him and put an announcement in the paper."

"Yikes. That's harsh. Not that he didn't deserve it, but Brandon should've at least been able to say goodbye to his father."

He brushed his hand against my forehead and leaned down to give me an avuncular peck on my lips. "Always thinking of others. You rest up today."

I grabbed his arm, the forearm I loved so much, and asked, "And tomorrow you break me out of this joint?"

"Well, this joint was your room, but yes, tomorrow we move your things to my room, where I can keep an eye on you."

"Keep an eye on me, huh? Keep telling yourself that." I smirked, and he kissed the smirk off my face.

$$25$$

The Reading of the Will

Marc

Kayleigh and Claire were up and ready to go by the time I got to the kitchen the next morning. Claire looked as if someone killed her puppy. While she was always a darker version of Kayleigh, with her dark hair and eyes, today her mood reflected her looks. In contrast, Kayleigh had a fake smile plastered on her face. She was buzzing around, wiping the immaculately clean kitchen counters.

I stayed her hand, threw the dishtowel in the sink, and asked, "What's the matter? Who do I need to beat up?"

Claire smiled at that, but Kayleigh stuttered, "D … d … dad is coming to the reading of the will."

Nodding, I pulled Kayleigh toward me. "Understandable. He's an heir and probably the largest one." Her breath released when I held her close, making me feel ten feet tall.

Kayleigh leaned against me and whispered in my chest, "He hasn't seen Claire since the accident."

Glancing over at Claire, I asked, "What? He never visited?"

Claire averted her eyes and shook her head. "Neither he nor my mom ever came to visit. He doesn't even pick up the phone when I call. He'll only respond to text messages and usually they're generic messages."

It was inexcusable, but I didn't want either of the Breaux girls to be downcast. "Well, he's old and lives out of state. Sometimes the older generation has trouble with the newfangled technology." It was a reach, and Claire clearly wasn't in the mood to excuse her dad for his atrocious behavior. "Or, he could just be a *tchu.*"

Kayleigh snorted, and Claire responded, "It's that last one. He only moved out of state a few months ago. He lived in Meauxville a half an hour from the hospital. That's okay. He's never been there for me. You, Kayleigh, have always been there for me."

"Damn straight, Breaux sisters united." They punched their fists together like the Wonder Twins on the old *Justice League* cartoon.

"Shape of a coffee cup." I said, just to lighten the mood. They both looked at me as if I was crazy. "I'm not that much older than you. Are you telling me you've never watched the *Justice League*?"

Kayleigh tilted her head to the side. "That long movie with Wonder Woman, yes. But I don't remember anyone saying they wanted to be the shape of a coffee cup."

"How old is he?" Claire stage whispered.

I poured my coffee and pointed to her. "Old enough to take you over my knee for being disrespectful."

Claire grinned. "You mean my sister, of course. Although, based on her blush, I would say that I don't think spanking her will deter her bad behavior."

I turned to Kayleigh. She was beet red. "Good to know." I said and took my coffee on to the porch while Kayleigh and Claire argued. When Kayleigh made her way to the porch, she sat beside me on the porch swing and then kissed my cheek. Then she snuggled up next to me, leaning on my shoulder, her soft curls tickling my neck. I kissed her head and breathed in her familiar scent of lavender.

"Thanks for taking Claire's mind off of my dad's terrible parenting," she said.

I wrapped my arm around her back and hugged her closer. "Doesn't sound like he parented at all. Sounds like you did all the parenting."

I felt her shrug her shoulders. "You do what has to be done."

My phone pinged, and I glanced at my screen. Armand had texted me.

> Armand: The family is meeting for breakfast before heading to the lawyers. Can you bring Kayleigh and Claire?

> We'll be there. Wait. Let me ask first.

> Armand: Good idea. My cousins don't take well to being ordered about.

> Talk about!

When I turned to Kayleigh, I saw she had been reading the messages over my shoulder.

She gave me a peck on the cheek. "We would love to meet everyone for breakfast."

"You wanna check with Claire?"

Kayleigh shrugged. "She said she wanted to go out for breakfast earlier. Tell them yes. And Marc—"

"Yes?"

She grinned and kissed me until I forgot what I was doing. Pulling away, she smiled and said, "Thanks for asking and not telling us."

With a blink, I remembered what I was doing. "I'm learning." I texted Armand back.

> It's a go on breakfast. Meet you there in thirty minutes?

At the restaurant, Armand gave Kayleigh and Claire a big hug before we sat down to eat.

"You nervous?" He asked them.

"Not me." Kayleigh told him. "All I care about is my family and my family is Claire."

"And me!" Armand told her.

"Us too!" Valerie told her. "We're all your cousins."

"Beats the family I had before we did the genetic testing." Kayleigh told them. "The one I was born into was *pas bon*."

"Well, we're great!" Tanner told her. He held up his hand like Tony the Tiger in a Kellogg's commercial.

That lightened the mood, and we all dug into our breakfasts. After breakfast, Shell's mama, Ms. Ellie Mae, took all the Littles, except Valerie, home to the Babineaux complex. Valerie was the oldest *Little* and asked to be included in the process.

The adults invited to the will reading all headed to Mr. William Breaux's lawyer's office, a Mr. Hebert, Esquire. As the reading of the will unfolded in Mr. Hebert's office, I made certain that Hercule Trahan was in attendance. Armed with the filed motions and Mr. Breaux's signed documents, Mr. Trahan safeguarded the money from being misappropriated by Mr. Breaux, even after his death. Hercule brought his son with him, Sheriff Bradley Trahan, to make sure everything was on the up and up. Each time Bill's lawyer deviated from the proper legal protocol, Hercule would interrupt, causing me to bite my lip to hold back my laughter. Meanwhile, Bradley took meticulous notes in his notebook, documenting the lawyer's missteps and consistently citing statutes pertaining to profiting from criminal behavior. It was an amusing game of badinage.

Mr. Hebert would spew such inanities as, "As per Mr. Breaux's wishes, all of his goods and belongings will be left to his only heir, Brandon Breaux. In addition, the funds he is managing for his brother will be put in trust to be managed by trustees appointed by Mr. Breaux."

Hercule would respond, "Now, Mr. Hebert, you know that would be an illegal use of means. Surely you are not suggesting that Mr. Breaux's breach of contract be upheld. Particularly since he tried to ensure that breach with the murder of his other family members that should legally inherit. Why, such a move could get you disbarred! Have you not received the copies of the motions I filed? In addition, I sent you a copy of the original will and the agreement that Mr. Breaux signed to get his grubby paws on his inheritance?"

Mr. Hebert stiffened. "Mr. Trahan, I am just reading the will, as it is stated. At the time of the writing, I had no knowledge of Mr. Breaux's illegal actions or intentions. Also, calling a dead man names such as grubby seems beneath you."

Mr. Trahan nodded. "Of course you're right. I will be more truthful and call him a homicidal sociopath. However, since you do now know of the legal impediments to Mr. Breaux's invalid will, why don't you let me proceed with the legal distribution of the assets?"

In the end, Kevin and Mr. Trahan revealed that Bill had made his brother sign an illegal deal so that he gained access to his half of the fortune. Kailey's father admitted to an extramarital affair, and that Bill had pictures and videos. That was how Bill got him to sign over his fortune. He didn't know the documents he signed were illegal, so he had been living off the 'kindness' of his brother. Bill had been controlling his fortune long before Claire and Kayleigh got in the wreck. By the end of the meeting, Kayleigh's dad split the money in three: one third for him and his wife, one third for Kayleigh, and one third for Claire. Once that was done, he left for Florida without another word to his daughters.

For the other half of the money, one half went to Bill's eldest male progeny, Armand. Bill Breaux's remaining funds were divided up in an equitable manner, ensuring that each of his remaining children and grandchildren—Valerie, Tanner, Bailey Marie, Aida, Blaise, and his legitimate son, Brandon—received an equal share.

When we came out of the meeting, Beau joked, "I guess that means I have fewer college funds to fund. My dad will have a field day investing these funds."

Valerie, having only understood a fraction of what happened, asked. "Daddy, can we go to the bookstore? We have more money for books, right?"

Shell giggled, "Yes, you are swimming in book funds now. Books for everyone!" We gathered the rest of the *Littles* and headed to Beausoleil Books.

After the bookstore and being the Book Sherpa for my household, I called my architect about adding a library to my house. Kayleigh must have overheard the conversations because she started sending me pictures of amazing library rooms and video clips of library songs from Disney's *Beauty and the Beast.*

26

Christmas Eve

Kayleigh

I wouldn't get the money for a while, but I decided to splurge anyway. I ordered a bunch of gifts for Marc, Sofia, and Claire. For my white elephant gift, I was determined to have my presents be the single present that Marc wanted for our Christmas Eve celebration with the Krewe.

"You know, we get to decide which present we keep. Someone else might claim that present," Claire said when I told her of my plan. I was fixing her hair for the candlelight Midnight Mass that we would all go to after our celebration at the Babineaux complex. We decided to have the celebration at Armand and Renee's home, *Mes Rêves*, since the twins were the hardest to transport.

"Nope. Marc will get it and love it. You'll see." I finished styling Claire's hair and opened the door when Sofia knocked. Sofia joined us as we prepared for the celebrations. It was girl time and Marc was only allowed in once we were all prepared. Sofia, with the help of my sister, was an adorable pastel goth now. We kept her hair black, because it was such a lovely black-blue color. Claire just sprayed the tips of her pigtails with the hot pink color. Claire had been practicing her fine motor skills by drawing with pastel metallic Sharpies on both her and Sofia's white Doc Martens. She and Claire even got matching tights, with Claire's being lilac and black, while Sofia's were pink and black. When Marc opened the door, he pressed his lips together as he looked us over.

As we got in the SUV to head to *Mes Rêves*, Marc mumbled into my ear. "I've lost any influence I had over her, haven't I?"

I bit my lower lip and his eyes flashed. "Not at all. You're just gonna need to work for it. Like everything else in your life from now on."

He snorted. "You sayin' I had it easy before you came along?"

"*Pourri gâté*, that's what you were. But no more being spoiled. No more easy living. You're gonna have to earn it." I leaned back against the seat.

He leaned down and whispered, "Oh! I'll earn it alright." My face flushed.

"Whatcha talking about, Daddy?" Sofia asked. My sister, bless her heart, distracted her. Marc's arm came around me, and I felt his silent chuckle. Looking up, I gave him a t'*bec doux*, on one of his dimples.

Leaning over, his breath tickled my ear. "More kisses and just more, later." With my head against his shoulder, I closed my eyes.

When we arrived at *Mes Rêves*, Renee greeted us at the door, holding one of the twins.

Claire asked. "Which one is that, Blaise or Aida?"

"This is Aida. Blaise naps, and she is up all the time." She opened the door wide for us, Marc rolled Claire in, and Sofia and I traipsed in after them with all our gifts.

Once I had set down our white elephant gifts, I asked Renee, "Can I hold her?"

"Yes, please. She's a giant baby, and even my arms get tired." Which was saying a lot since Renee used to be a star softball pitcher, and Armand had nicknamed her Valkyrie. I grabbed up

Aida and made my way to the living room to sit in the recliner with her.

When I got there, Marc was at my side. "Let me help you with her." He scooped Aida out of my arms while I sat down in the recliner. Then he placed her in my arms and kissed me.

I smiled at him. "Can I answer your question now?"

"Later, you're busy with this little angel." He patted Aida on the head and she roared.

"Nice work!" I put her to my shoulder and patted her tush, frowning at Marc.

"See, not the time to accept a marriage proposal. We have time. After all, you're already married to me."

"You never did tell me how you managed to do that," I said as I soothed Aida.

"Let's just say money talks."

Shaking my head, I stage whispered to Aida, "*Nonc Marc est pas bon.*"

He leaned down and breathed into my ear. "Untrue. I'm very *bon*. I think you can attest to how good I am." A shiver ran through my body at that, and I closed my eyes and bit my lip. He smiled against my ear. "I see you remember."

"None of that!" Renee walked into the living room. "This is a PG-rated celebration."

Shell, who followed her, asked, "Why not a G-rated?"

Renee turned to her. "You think I can get the Krewe to not cuss in French?"

I snickered and kissed Aida on the head. "We'll teach you so you can cuss back at them, sweetie." She smiled up at me.

Once everyone but the sleeping babies had gathered in the living room, we distributed numbers. Marc got the first gift. He did not go for my gift, but I didn't worry about that. My gift was chosen as the third gift opened. Beau opened it, guffawed, and looked up at me. I pressed my lips together. Contrary to the rules, he showed it only to Shell who giggled and to Armand, who was next in line to select. He grabbed up the gift and, like Beau, only showed it to the next in line.

Valerie, who might one day be a lawyer, complained, with all her tweenage angst, "You're not following the rules!" However, when it was her turn, Gelly, who couldn't stop giggling, showed her the gift. She turned to me and shook her head. I bit my lips.

"What's going on? You can't all want the same gift. Let me see. I'm next in line," Marc said.

Valerie shook her head, and Gelly quickly hid the gift behind her back.

Claire, knowing all along what was happening, asked him. "You want a new gift or to steal someone else's?"

"I want the gift that is making everyone laugh. Hand it over." He extended his hand and Gelly looked to Valerie, who nodded. Valerie placed the Christmas ornament in his hands.

Marc frowned. "It's a very nice ornament, but I don't see what's so funny."

"Look closer, Sherlock!" Claire said.

Marc squinted and then pulled some folded reading glasses from his shirt pocket.

"Old man," Etienne coughed.

Marc scoffed. "It just so happens I read a lot." And then he read the ornament.

Dear Marc,
Stop ducking me.
Yes, I will marry you.
Now, ask me already.
Love,
Kayleigh

Marc's eyes met mine and his grin was wide enough that his dimples popped out. Then he went over to the tree and pulled out his box. Written on the present was, 'For Kayleigh Only'.

He handed it to me, and I ripped open the gift.

Valerie, ever the arbiter of fairness, complained. "It's not your turn."

"Tough." We both told her in chorus.

Inside the box was another poison ring. This one had a flat top with our initials engraved on it.

"Look inside." He told me.

Opening the ring, I saw a picture of him and Sofia on one side and Claire and myself on the other. I swallowed, trying to talk.

"Wait, don't talk yet." He held his hand out to the side, and Sofia took it. "Kayleigh Isabelle Breaux," he said.

Sofia interrupted. "Will you marry my daddy and become my mama?"

Claire grabbed my hand. "So we can be one big family?"

I couldn't talk through the tears. I heard Tanner ask his sister, "Val, are these good tears or bad tears?"

"Shh ... good tears," Val told him.

I grabbed Marc's free hand and asked, "What about your stupid relationship agreement?"

With that, Marc pulled out our relationship agreement from his jacket and tore it up. "I love you, not for a reciprocal benefit or because you will make a great mother, but because you are you. Now, will you stop being a pain in my *tchu* and marry me already?"

I pulled my hands away and put them on my hips. "Hey, I'm not the one being difficult."

Claire rolled her eyes, and Sofia put her hand up. "Daddy, do you love Kayleigh?"

"Didn't I just say that?" Marc frowned.

"Answer the question with a yes or a no," Claire said, channeling *Law and Order*.

"Yes."

Sofia turned to me. "Ms. Kayleigh, do you love my daddy and me?"

Sighing, I said, "Yes, with all my heart."

"Then I pronounce you both officially engaged. Stop fighting," Sofia said.

"You can kiss now," Claire added.

I closed my eyes and chuckled. When I opened them, Marc was there, right in front of me. "I love you, Kayleigh."

"I love you, too." With that, he kissed me and slipped the ring on my finger.

⚜

27

Christmas Lovin'

Marc

Once we got back from the party, we tag teamed Sofia and Claire. While I read a story to Sofia from her basket of Christmas stories, Kayleigh worked with Claire on some cloved oranges. I know it sounded odd, but apparently reaching in and picking up the cloves was helping Claire's fine motor skills. Plus, it gave her alone time with her sister and made our house smell like a Christmas orange grove. After a half hour, we switched. Kayleigh read a story from the basket of French books to Sofia, while Claire and I discussed her progress and her medical needs. Claire had asked for this time because Kayleigh got emotional and fretted if Claire was not making progress. Claire's desire to relieve her sister's worry did not waver, even as she remained focused on her therapy and life goals.

"So how's it going, my soon-to-be sis?" I ruffled her hair. She was a sweet kid.

"My fine motor skills in my hand are gradually improving. However, if I intend to apply to Louisiana University's art program next fall, it might be wise to have a backup plan. Have you heard of mouth painting?"

I sat next to her bed on the recliner and lay back. "I've heard of *My Left Foot*. Where that painter used his foot to paint."

Claire nodded. "Similar principal. My mouth is working great. Probably to keep up with my snarky sister."

I patted her shoulder. "No doubt a survival skill with her. I could use some pointers."

She chuckled, "Yes, one has to be on their feet to brawl with Kay Kay."

"Understood. So, you need a tutor to help you learn to mouth paint?" I sat in the rocking recliner next to her bed and leaned back in it, focusing on the ceiling. Sometimes, I got more of a response from Claire with my gaze averted.

"Yes, please," she singsonged. "I've started on my own, but I need some help. I need pointers and techniques."

"Well, since you asked so politely—"

"—Polar opposite of Kay Kay, right?" Claire laughed.

I guffawed and texted a note to my office manager. "I'll have a tutor for you right after Christmas. Does that work for you?"

"Besides breaking me out of that nasty, starve-me, assisted dying facility, it's the best gift I've ever gotten."

Pulling the recliner lever, I sat up and patted Claire's hand. "Stick around, kid. There's more where that came from."

"I hope that Kayleigh keeps you around. I really like you Marc," she said, snuggling under her covers the best she could.

"Back at ya, kiddo." I grabbed the quilt at the bottom of her bed and covered her with it. When I was sure she was comfortable, I patted her foot through the blankets as I exited the room.

Once we had gotten the "minors," as Kayleigh called them, to sleep, we situated ourselves on the living room floor. Kayleigh put on Micheal Doucet and Beausoleil's *Christmas Bayou* album and we sampled Sofia's famous peanut butter, oatmeal, and chocolate chip cookies. Sofia had left a sweet spread for *Papa Noël*. Since we were finishing wrapping presents, we figured we were Santa's minions and deserved a portion of his snacks.

After an hour, I had an epiphany. "I believe I may have purchased too many gifts."

Kayleigh snickered. "No, I'm sure most kids get about twenty presents for Christmas. Can we stop wrapping now?" She rubbed and rotated her wrist. "I think I'm getting carpel tunnel. You can save some for other events, you know. They won't care. What's important is that we'll be spending time with them."

"Let's do that then. Come with me." I pulled her up from the floor and led her to my room. "Look what I did, for days that we don't want to leave the room at all." In the corner of my bedroom, I had installed a coffee station.

"You put a kitchenette in your room?" She explored the various coffee pods, smiling when she saw the hot chocolate.

"More of a coffee-slash-snack station. Look, this is where you recycle the pods and under here is your milk, annnnd." I pulled out a bottle from my mini-fridge and showed it to her like a sommelier or Vanna White.

"Eggnog, yay! The perfect post-Christmas wrapping beverage." She grabbed up two large mugs from the coffee station, and I poured us each a mug of eggnog. From there, we moved to the sofa in my sitting area to relax.

After the first sweet spicy sip, I turned to Kayleigh. "Tell me about your family. What were your Christmases like growing up? Claire seems so happy and well-adjusted, but she sure doesn't ask for much, and you haven't asked for anything."

"I just want Claire happy and healthy. For most of my life, that's been my life's goal. Our Christmases differed diametrically from yours, I'm sure. Ms. Sue and Mr. Lionel are warm, fuzzy, happy Christmas types."

"Indeed, they were. Dad played Santa until I was eleven and figured out it was him. Mom and Mawmaw were always cooking every treat imaginable in the kitchen. I try to carry on the tradition with Sofia. Although the cooking is because of Chef Agnès."

"You're a wonderful father, and Agnès is an amazing chef. Myself, I always tried to make Christmas special for Claire. When we were younger, I remember my parents going to parties, but we never decorated the house and we didn't have any family celebrations. Christmas was for them. When I got older and they left me alone for their yearly Christmas Cruise, I tried to make it special for Claire. Once I was hired as a librarian, I went all out decorating and creating events for all the kids. One never knew if that would be their only holiday celebration, so I wanted to make it count."

"We'll make it special for both Claire and Sofia, and I hope to make it special for you." I squeezed her knee.

She leaned against my shoulder and sighed. "You and the Krewe already have."

My arm encircled her. "No, *I* want to make it special, just for you."

She placed her mug on the nightstand, and the side of her mouth twitched up. "That sounds promising. Whadya have in mind?"

My hand reached towards her. I hesitated and, in the end, simply brushed a golden lock behind her ear. That simple touch made my heart jolt and my pulse pound.

"Cat got your tongue?" Kayleigh teased.

My retort caught in my throat. Instead, I swooped in and kissed her. My hungry, ravishing kisses slowed to drugging kisses as my tongue traced her plump, rosebud mouth. Her fingers whispered into my hair, pulling and dragging me closer. Without breaking the kiss, I twisted so that Kayleigh straddled me. My hands gripped her hips, positioning her warmth. I felt that warmth against my all too ready member. Kayleigh rocked against me and moaned.

I pulled back, trying to reposition her. "You're killing me here!"

She leaned forward, nipped my earlobe, and murmured, "You want me to stop?"

"God, no!"

Her smile brushed against my ear while her small hands began unbuttoning my shirt. Two can play at that game. I tried to unbutton her shirt, but my traitorous hands wouldn't stop shaking. I gave up and just ripped with both hands. Buttons flew in all directions, revealing her perfect little breasts, but Kayleigh groused.

"Hey, I liked that shirt."

I nipped her ear. "I'll buy you five more." As I moved in, she feinted left and rolled off the sofa.

Grasping the two ends of her shirt together, she said, "I can buy my own damn clothes." Then stormed out of the room. *What the?* Confused and aroused, I followed in her wake when she slammed her door in my face.

Not wanting my daughter as an audience, I tapped at Kayleigh's door, whispering, "Kayleigh, I'm sorry."

When she didn't respond, I tried again and then a third time. Finally, Kayleigh opened her door a crack and asked, "Sorry for what?"

Good question. I tried to think back through my lust-shrouded brain. *What had gone wrong?* She stormed off after I ripped her shirt, and then I offered to buy shirts for her. I took a chance and picked.

"I'm sorry for ripping your shirt?"

"Wrong."

"I'm sorry for offering to replace the shirt I ripped?"

"Closer."

"Kayleigh, can you please give me a break? I'm sure I said something stupid, but in my defense, you have perfect breasts."

The door swung open. "That's your defense?" Kayleigh was standing there with the inside curve of her breasts on full display. I grinned, and she followed my eyes. "Hey, eyes up here, Richard. I'm telling you now for the last time. I don't need your money. I can survive and even take care of Claire without you. I'm a strong, independent woman. You think because I had to live in my car for a little while that I'm weak? I'm stronger than you ever could imagine. I pay my own way, period."

"Of course you do. Your strength of spirit is why I know you will make a great mother for Sofia. You were willing to live in your car rather than do the wrong thing. That shows strength of character."

She studied me for a moment, and finally nodded. "Okay." She backed up and motioned for me to go into her room.

Her scent, lavender, cinnamon, and Kayleigh infused the air. I grinned and moved towards her. She pulled on my arm and led me to her bed. I opened my mouth to tell her how lovely she was, but she put her finger over my lips.

"Ah, ah, I'm going to have to take certain measures for us to pull this off." She moved behind me, searching through her dresser drawers, and said over her shoulder, "Take off your clothes, please."

She did not have to tell me twice. I shrugged out of my shirt and wriggled out of my pants.

"Commando. Good to know," she said from right behind my ear. She had climbed on the bed as I undressed. A scarf came across my mouth.

"Heyy." I said, or tried to.

"You want to chance saying something *couillon* again?" I shook my head, and she nipped my ear from behind. "Smart choice. Now lay back. No talking."

I pulled off the scarf.

"Hey!" She frowned.

But I put my finger in front of my mouth and shook my head. Promising not to speak.

"You promise not to talk?" she asked.

I nodded.

She smirked. "We'll see. You may proceed."

To keep from talking and saying anything that might annoy her, I kept my mouth busy. Nipping at her ultra sensitive ears, then sucking down her neck, I wanted to spend enough time there to force her to wear a turtleneck for the celebrations tomorrow. Yes, I was juvenile and possessive. When I reached her perfectly pert breasts, she moaned. I shushed her. If I had to be quiet, then she did too. I cupped them, sucking and rolling that rosy nipple between my tongue and teeth. She was doing a piss-poor job of staying quiet. I grinned against her breast.

She must have noticed because she whacked me on my head. "Stop messing around."

I flipped her over and made my way down her body. My mouth licked from her breasts to her core. Moving her thighs apart, I situated myself between them. With lips, and tongue, and teeth, I worked her over as my fingers delved into her. Waiting for the telltale spasms. She gasped, and I relished her fall, and in that instant I was in her. As we rode her aftershocks, I gasped and pumped. She settled and then rose again. I held back, wanting to hold her on the brink of bliss. I counted backwards. I sang the Star-Spangled Banner. I tried to remember my brutal first grade teacher that hated me. Nothing worked. I reached between us, searching for the little pearl that could lift my Kayleigh over the edge. She inhaled, arched, and moaned. I let myself go after that, crushing and reclaiming her mouth as she swallowed my roar. I awoke on top of Kayleigh with her rubbing my back.

"What happened to 'Safety First. Safety Always?'" she asked when she noticed I was awake.

"You're safe. You're here with me."

"Umm hmm," was all she said.

Confused, I rolled off her to take care of the condom. "Oh." She snickered. I should have panicked, but I only felt lightness. "Maybe we should talk about family and children?"

Kayleigh snorted as I made my way back to bed. "We should. We definitely should, but not right now." She reached for me.

28

Christmas Day

Kayleigh

I woke the next morning, Christmas morning, snuggled next to Marc, a warm naked Marc. The sound and smells of Christmas beckoned. I squirmed to leave the bed, but Marc caught me and pulled me to him. As he pulled me against him, I inhaled his soapy scent and absorbed his warmth.

"Not yet. Stay." His words tickled my ear, and I smiled.

When his hand cupped my breast, I decided I could wait a few minutes before I left the bed. Marc rolled on top of me and confirmed that was a wise decision. His hand traced down my body, from my face to my shoulders to my breasts, and beyond.

"Your parents are coming. Mine might be too. They might already be here." I whispered.

Marc's dimples emerged, and he leaned closer to murmur in my ear. "In that case, you will need to use that pillow to keep the noise down." Then he rose back above me and gave my body a raking gaze, causing all my nerve endings to tingle in anticipation. His warm, large hands explored my body, following his gaze. His mouth claimed my lips and made its way down my body, tugging and nibbling on my nipples. With my attention diverted, his hand slid across my belly and between my thighs. I was slick with desire as his caresses focused on my sensitive bud. Electricity seared across my nerves, and I pulled him closer.

"More." I told him. "No more playing around."

He lifted. His dimples were on full display. "You're sure?"

"Less talk, more action." I arched my back so that my breast lifted and my nipple brushed against his lips.

He licked and said, "We live in a litigious society. Verbal confirmation, please."

"Stop tormenting me. Yes, more, please!"

"Since you asked so politely." He shifted, moving a knee between my legs. His hand that had been tormenting me dipped one finger and then another inside of me, stretching me. He reached for the nightstand drawer and pulled out a condom. Slipping it on in no time flat. His mouth met mine for drugging kisses. His tongue slipping inside overwhelmed my senses. I could feel him pushing into me, filling me. Not like before, when he had been teasing me. He stopped when I tensed, distracting me with kisses or caressing my breasts. If this was to ease or slow the process, then he miscalculated, because those distractions only made me squirm and increased his torment exponentially. In an instant, it happened. Marc's control snapped. He rode a wave of desire as he pistoned his hips and crushed his mouth on mine. His hand slipped between us to caress that nub, sending tingles through my nerves, lifting me higher and higher. A moment later, we both shattered and collapsed on the bed. His crushing weight felt reassuring, and my legs twined around his lower back to keep him in place.

Marc had proven the night before that he was a flopper, so once we had our 'Christmas present', as he called it, he conked out on top of me. With my eyes closed, I took a brief moment to relish his soapy scent and the feel of his skin. I got out of bed and threw on my warm, fuzzy robe. I made my way to the family room to hang out with whoever was already up and moving. On the way out the door, I caught sight of myself. *No frickin' way!* Angling my neck to the side, I spotted a mark there. No, not just any mark. A hickey. I glowered at Marc's inert form.

"You *t'tchu!*" I muttered, because he was a little ass. With detailed visions of how I'd make Marc pay, I made a beeline to my room. I needed to find something to wear to hide my neck from his parents, Claire, and Sofia.

When I finally arrived in the family room, Sofia was occupied with shaking presents for both herself and Claire. Sofia shook the present next to Claire's ear, and they both took turns guessing what was inside. The smell of coffee and sweets drew me into the kitchen. In the kitchen, besides Chef Agnès, Marc's parents had arrived with their Christmas bounty. They turned when they heard me, but I wasn't looking at them.

"Oh, my God! Y'all do a *Croquembouche à Noël*! If I had known that, I would've gotten engaged to Marc much sooner."

"See," Ms. Sue snickered and stage whispered to her husband, "I told you we should've mentioned the *Croquembouche*!"

"As usual, you were right, my love." Mr. Lionel patted her shoulder. "Here, try some sampler profiteroles, you know, for quality control."

I snatched the sweets from Mr. Lionel and the coffee that Chef Agnès was holding for me. "This alone makes this the best Christmas I've ever had. Thank you!" I went to the living room to split my booty with my sister and Sofia. While we sampled the chocolate-filled profiteroles, my phone buzzed. I figured it was my parents. Marc had invited them to Christmas. Claire was sure they would come. I think she thought that they were absent because of Nonc Bill. But alas, no.

"Mom and Dad can't make it." I told Claire, hoping she'd leave it at that.

"Why not? What happened?" she asked.

"Nothing, they just can't make it," I hedged.

Claire looked at Sofia. "You can read people. True or not true?"

Sofia examined me, tilted her head, and said, "Not completely true."

"Fine. They're going on their annual Christmas cruise, but it doesn't matter, because we finally have an actual family this year. A family that cares about us, to celebrate with for Christmas."

"I always had a family for Christmas," Claire said. "You were always there for me."

"And I always will be there for you, but now you have an even bigger family."

"Like me!" Sofia told her.

"And me." Marc said, walking into the living room in his Christmas themed PJs.

"Told ya, Claire, this will be the best Christmas yet. Wait until you see the *Croquembouche*!" My arms encircled her, and I laid my head on her shoulder.

"A *Croquembouche*! Why didn't you marry Marc sooner?"

"If I'd known it was that easy, I would've told you sooner." Marc snarked.

"No, if I'd have succumbed, you'd have labeled me a 'pastry digger' and written in some clause into the relationship agreement about how many pastries I'm allowed to eat."

He walked over, grabbed me in a bear hug and murmured in my ear, "You can sample all my pastries."

I chuckled, "Good to know and expect me to collect on that."

"Ugh!" Claire said, "No PDA in the living room. It's present opening time. Let's get this show on the road!"

The entire family gathered in the living room for the festivities. The Christmas decorations were perfect with the trees, wreaths, ornaments, and stacks and stacks of wrapped presents. But that wasn't why my throat clenched. It was the warmth, and the smiles, and most of all, the love. Sofia's arm was intertwined with Claire's. Ms. Sue had her head on Mr. Lionel's shoulder, and Marc's eyes were trained on me.

Marc reached over and cupped my chin. "You ready to get this show on the road?" I nodded and kissed him as he smiled against my lips.

"Ugh, PDA." Sofia said, mimicking Claire.

We broke apart chuckling, and Mr. Lionel started passing out the presents. Claire and Sofia got art supplies, clothes, and plenty of books. In fact, everyone got a variety of different presents except for me. I kept opening up presents with one singular theme.

"Ah, a Kevlar jacket. This matches my Kevlar t-shirt, and my collection of Kevlar vests."

Claire snickered. "It's your own fault. If you hadn't gotten yourself shot, you might've gotten something like a book for Christmas."

"That's not all I got her!" Marc complained.

"Yes, dear," Ms. Sue cooed. "You also gifted her with her very own can of mace, and the lovely purple taser—"

Mr. Lionel finished for his wife. "—and the brass knuckles keychain. Very romantic."

I pressed my lips together, because in its own way, it *was* romantic.

"Those are not my only gifts. He pulled out an envelope from his pocket."

"What's this?" I turned the envelope over in my hands.

"This is for our honeymoon. My parents already agreed to watch over Claire and Sofia while we're on our trip."

I opened the envelope, and my mouth dropped open. "What is this?" There were tickets to six different locations.

"Start with this one and guess." He handed me the airline ticket to Egypt, along with a train ticket to Alexandria.

"The Biblioteca Alexandria! We are going to the site of the world's first library!"

"And in first class, to boot!" Marc added.

"Oh, who cares how we get there? Oh, oh, oh, tickets to Rome! The Vatican Library. We can go see the *Codex Vaticanus,* the first biblical manuscript from the 4th century!"

"Yes, sounds like fun." Marc chuckled and rolled his eyes.

"You've no one to blame but yourself. You knew she was a nerd when you married her for convenience, and even after that, you chose to marry her for real." Claire told him.

"—Oh, oh, oh! *La Bibliothèque nationale de France*. They've the most beautiful illuminated manuscripts from the middle ages. Wait 'til you see them. The British library. We get to see the *Magna Carta!*" At this point, I was jumping up and down.

"Yippee!" Marc teased.

I elbowed him. "It'll be fun, then back to the States for the Library of Congress and the New York Public Library. Best trip ever! When can we leave?"

"The best time for me is after Mardi Gras. My company has a lot of work during that holiday, keeping people safe. Once Lent starts, the workload goes down and I can have my second in charge run the show. Can you get off then?"

"I'll schedule my vacation days for that time. Two weeks?" I pulled out my phone to schedule the trip.

"Better make it three."

With a swipe, I opened the calendar on my phone and asked, "Which means we marry when?"

Marc grinned, dimples showing. "Epiphany."

✦

Epilogue: King Cake

Marc

For the twelve days of Christmas, I worked to make sure that both Kayleigh and Claire felt at home. I followed the overarching themes of *The Twelve Days of Christmas* song, these included trees, birds, and music. The day after Christmas, I asked the Breaux sisters their favorite fruit and planted two trees in our orchard in the secret garden. Kayleigh selected fig as her favorite and Claire selected satsuma. Leading up until Epiphany, I asked their favorite birds and created a habitat for those birds on my ... our land. For Kayleigh, that meant hummingbird feeders and hummingbird friendly plants. Since we already had the plants, I just added a feeder where she could see it from their reading folly. Claire, in contrast, loved owls. That entailed more work. I put in nesting boxes, put the outdoor night lights on timers, and installed a fountain bird bath. Then I asked them what music they listened to, liked to play, or wanted to learn to play. Claire was easy. She just wanted a keyboard and lessons. Easy peasy and it helped with her physical therapy. Kayleigh decided she wanted to learn to play the fiddle. By day three of her lessons, we had moved her to an exterior building, and my men were allowed to guard her from the outside or wearing ear plugs. I grinned as I thought about her lessons. My ears would never be the same.

I headed to our family room with my head full of thoughts of the upcoming ceremony. To prepare for our guests, our housekeeper was packing away the Christmas ornaments from the pine tree. I worked on the gold tree to give her a *coup de main* or helping hand.

"Daddy, you can't take down the gold tree. That's the Mardi Gras tree!" Sophia warned me as I replaced red Christmas decorations with purple Epiphany/Mardi Gras decorations.

"I'm not, *Chèrie*. I'm just pulling off all the red ornaments. Go grab the box in the garage marked 'Mardi Gras' and you and Claire can help put up the new ornaments."

"I'll select and you put them up," Claire said. She was able to maneuver her motorized chair herself, using her developing fine motor skills. The PT she had been doing and the new stem cell treatments were working to get her added mobility and use of her hands. We were working on fine motor skills now.

Together, we transformed the decorations from the red, green, and gold of Christmas into the vibrant purple, green, and gold of Mardi Gras. This way, we set the stage for the festive feast of the kings and the upcoming Mardi Gras season.

"Where's Kayleigh?" I asked Claire. "Did she practice her fiddle today? You know she wouldn't want to miss this." One thing I knew for certain about Kayleigh was her eagerness to join in decorating activities, regardless of what they were.

"You can't see her until the ceremony," Sofia said primly, wrapping the red ornaments and placing them in the box marked 'Christmas Decorations'.

I grimaced a bit as the box brought back memories of our fight. However, that was behind us. We had donated the offending decorations to charity and besides, as Kayleigh reminded me, if it hadn't been for that lying, cheating bitch, Tracy, we wouldn't have Sofia. So, the betrayal was one hundred percent worth it. With a gaze at my lovely daughter, I smiled over at her ensemble. Sofia had a bright purple velvet dress with her signature black Pippi Longstocking braids with green tips and gold Doc Martens. She'd be the perfect Mardi Gras flower girl.

"Yes, I must always follow the rules," I said, but I scanned the hall for a glimpse of Kayleigh, who was peaking around the corner admiring our decorations.

"Actually," Claire corrected, "the rule is that you can't see the dress." She followed my gaze and waved at her sister.

Sofia frowned. "Are you sure?"

Claire shrugged. "I think so. Let's look it up." She let Sofia roll her out of the room to research wedding customs and lore.

Kayleigh snuck into the family room. She grinned at the Mardi Gras tree and walked over to kiss my cheek. "Father LeBrun will be here soon for the convalidation ceremony."

"Yes." I pulled her towards me, my hands stroking her back and pressing her against me. Probably a mistake since my body, more accurately specific parts of it, became immediately rigid.

She squirmed against me, making it worse. "We can't do anything until then."

I pouted and heaved a sigh. "I know." We had been taking courses with Father LeBrun, and it was killing me.

She leaned forward and breathed into my ear. "But tonight, I move to your room permanently."

I grinned against her temple. "Finally. It can't come soon enough."

She stilled, and I pulled back to look at her. "What's wrong?" I asked.

"Do you think Mr. Lionel minds walking me down the aisle? I really thought that after everything my parents would come around, but they couldn't even be bothered to make it to our wedding."

"He's honored, Kayleigh. Don't worry. He already considers you and Claire as family."

She leaned against my chest. "You really lucked out with your family and friends, you know that?"

"They're your family and friends as well." With that, I leaned towards her and reclaimed her lips, searing a path from her soft, warm lips to her earlobe. Right when things were getting interesting, the sound of the doorbell shattered the moment, preventing us from getting into any good trouble. Kayleigh grinned up at me, her worries assuaged.

"Gotta get back to it. I want you to trip over your tongue when you see me." She skipped back to her room, tossing a saucy grin over her shoulders as she went. "See you soon. I'll be the one in the fancy dress."

We held the ceremony outside, under the live oaks. My Krewe acted as my groomsmen, with Beau serving as my best man. Unfortunately, his *Call of Duty* skills had declined due to having five children and no time to practice. The *Call of Duty* loser always earned the spot as best man, because it entailed coming up with a speech. Kayleigh had Renee as her maid of honor, and Shell, Gelly, and her sister, Claire, served as bridesmaids. My dad walked Kayleigh down the aisle. She resembled a princess in her strapless, lacy gold dress. I still got steamed that her parents couldn't make it because they were on a long cruise.

Kayleigh was grateful. "My father never lifted a finger for me. Mr. Lionel has been more of a father to me in the past few months than my own dad in all the years that I've known him." Luckily, my dad had a hankie in his pocket.

"I love you, Kayleigh girl." He told her and kissed her cheek.

"I love you too, Mr. Lionel." At that, my dad was wiping his eyes as we walked away.

The theme of our wedding was Mardi Gras, as it was held on the twelfth night of Christmas. We had small king cakes at each table and a larger one for us to cut. Our colors were the Mardi Gras colors of gold, green, and purple. Kayleigh's favorite colors. Our first dance was to Cedric Watson's version of the "La Vieille

Chanson de Mardi Gras." And for our wedding meal, we served red beans and rice and corn bread, along with all the side dishes and desserts that our friends and family brought. It was simple, fun, stress-free, and delicious. Renee and Beau had short and sweet toasts and Kayleigh agreed to sneak off with me once her dress was covered in cash. Not that we needed the cash, but she had promised the library to donate that money for new books.

"Can we leave now?" I grumbled. Once I was finally able to pry Kayleigh away from everyone that wanted to dance with her, I pulled her behind an old live oak.

She snickered. "You getting restless? I still have an empty section here." Kayleigh pointed to a small section where her dress was still visible through the cash.

I pulled out my wallet, grabbed some hundreds, and covered up any conceivable blank area. "It is time for us to leave." I pulled her arm and led her to our house. She laughed and followed me. At the door, I lifted her up, crossed the threshold, and then tried not to run, full speed, to our room.

"In a hurry?" She asked, playing with my hair.

"Nope. Not at all," I said and bounced her onto the bed and followed in her wake, kissing her once I landed on top of her. Not letting up until my heartbeat felt hers. Her legs crossed on my back, pulled me closer to her heat. My heart pounded. The erratic thudding drowned out the music and frivolity from the reception. Seizing both of Kayleigh's wrists in one hand, I lifted them to the brass bedposts. I pulled up the leather cuffs I had put there earlier.

Kayleigh stilled. "Whatcha doing?"

"Remember when I said I would handcuff you, and then you shivered?" I attached the second cuff, so both of her hands were engaged.

"No."

"Hmm." I nibbled on her earlobe and skimmed my hand over her breasts through her dress. "Your nipples appear to remember. Your mouth votes 'no', but your breasts vote, 'yes'. Let's see what the rest of your body wants." I eased her body to its side. "Any discomfort?"

"No, but I reserve the right to call an end to this." She moaned when I licked across her shoulders as I undid the corset of her dress.

I tore it off of her, nearly losing my mind over the pastel blue confection it revealed. "*Mais, là*"

"Surprise!" Kayleigh smirked and wiggled. "I needed something blue, so we ordered lingerie from the Trashy Diva."

"Stop moving. Let me recover." My hands skimmed over the silk.

Kayleigh grinned. Her hot gaze traveled over me. "I love your hands on me." She arched into my touch. Looking me in the eye, she ordered, "Faster."

I pulled away, ripping at my clothes. Kayleigh's grin widened.

"You're not getting your way, you know." I taunted.

"We'll see. I betcha I do." Her eyes followed my every move.

After I had divested myself of my clothes, I put my hands back on her. She closed her eyes and moaned.

I breathed into her ear. "What is it you want, *mon amour*?"

"You inside me, now."

With one hand encircling her neck, I crushed my mouth onto hers. At first, urgent and hard, I slowed to drugging kisses. Until she relaxed, then I licked a path down her neck and shoulders. My touch alternated from light and teasing to hard and desperate. Still, I did not give her what she wanted. Not yet. When her nipples were taut and sensitive, I kept another hand teasing and caressing them as I moved further, kissing down her body. She pulled against her constraints and wrapped her legs around my torso, trying to push me up her body.

"Now!" she ordered.

I lifted my head and smirked. "Definitely not getting your way." Lowering my mouth to her core, I chuckled against her labia and she shivered. *That's what I'm talking about.* I got to work, licking, as first one finger, then another entered her. My tongue worked over her clit until she moaned. I pulled away, only to return and do it again. Because I could. Only for her to growl, the final time I did that, and pull me back in with her thighs. Smiling, I let her rise and caressed that pearl until she exploded. Until all that touched the bed as she moaned were her heels and her captive wrists.

I released her wrists and placed her serene form the way I wanted it. Admiring her calm, contented form, I spread her legs, entering her slowly. Kayleigh did a quick inhale and her walls closed around me. I closed my eyes, trying to think of something else, anything else. Kayleigh was having none of that.

"Look at me, Marc."

I opened my eyes, and there she was, my sunshine, my Tink. I watched as her eyes rolled back and groaned as her petal soft walls fluttered around me. It was all too much, and I began pumping in earnest. She matched me stroke for stroke until she went off like a roman candle. I focused on her face as she erupted, and in that instant, I followed her over.

As I laid over her, exhausted, replete, she tittered. "Told you I would get my way."

With a snort, I released her, rolled us both over, and slapped her ass. "In this, always." She lifted her head, kissed me softly, and laid against me and sighed. I fell asleep with her enfolded in my arms. *Safe. Mine.*

If you'd like to read more stories about Meauxville, try out the first book in the Babineaux Brother series: Bayou Catfish. Just scan the QR code on the next page.

Also by Gigi Hodge

Louisiana L'Amour Series

Learning to Love: Book 1
Dance of Love: Book 2
Thrown into Love: Book 3
Noël in Love: Book 4
Storm of Love (Novella)
Louisiana L'Amour Omnibus

Louisiana Small Town Romance

The Magic of Chemistry

The Babineaux Brothers

Bayou Catfish

About the Author

G rowing up in French Louisiana, Gigi was always a reader. But writing also played a role in her life once she began teaching. She worked with the National Writing project as a teacher and then helped to run a program as a professor. She participated in several Nanowrimo experiences (write a novel in a month) throughout the years. However, after she retired in November 2022, she finally listened to her inner voice and challenged herself to become a published writer.

Important to note: Since Gigi now lives abroad, she often uses her writing to connect to her home and experiences in Louisiana. Most of the restaurants and food in her work are not fictional places, although some of them have closed. Go eat there ... you will appreciate the Louisiana cuisine. Coming from a French Louisiana background, Gigi also includes the occasional French word or expression. She plans to create a Louisiana French bookmark to highlight her most used Cajun/Creole vocabulary.

Acknowledgements

No author is an island. It takes a team to pull together a book. I want to thank mine. So, thanks to my beta readers, Rebecca Klug and Nicole Boudreaux whose insights have been invaluable. I want to thank Holly Schullo for giving me a free line edit, best author gift ever. I also want to thank the All Write Well team for their support and instruction to help me learn how to move from being a hobby writer into a published author.

9 798990 464490